S0-AJD-363

CURRIC Juvenile J MUE
Muehl, Lois Baker.
The hidden year of Devlin
  Bates

THE
HIDDEN
YEAR of
DEVLIN
BATES

THE
HIDDEN
YEAR of
DEVLIN
BATES

by

LOIS
MUEHL

illustrated by JOHN MARTINEZ

HOLIDAY HOUSE • NEW YORK

To Our Sons

mue Sons

B
R
I
A

TORSTEN

Copyright © 1967 by Lois Baker Muehl
PRINTED IN THE UNITED STATES OF AMERICA

Contents

chapter I

Just an Oddball

"Hey, Dev, wait up, will ya?"

Not on your life. Even for Walt Selding, he wouldn't wait, any more than he'd hang around a hill of stinging ants. He was through with stupid fifth grade, through with school where you couldn't just sit and watch thunderheads boil into a gray Iowa sky, couldn't take a deep breath without choking on chalk dust. Now he was clear of that torture trap for the whole summer, Dev ran to escape it and the pack of laughing, shouting kids.

But Jim Rothman, with legs springy as a praying mantis, covered ground faster than Dev and jerked him to a halt with a stranglehold across the windpipe.

"Walt said you should wait, Bates." Jim's soft voice didn't match his grip.

"Aw, let him go." Walt puffed up, slowed by the weight of daily afternoon trips to the Malt Shop, and then the bakery. "Just wanted to ask, Dev—you coming out for Little League?"

Dev grabbed for any reason they might accept. "Didn't sign up in time."

"Your sister said you didn't try." Jim raked his fingers into

Dev's hair, yanked. "You're lying. What's your real reason?"

Dev froze, still as a rabbit trying to test discovery. Nikki blabbed everything! Well, he wouldn't tell—no matter what Jim did to force it out of him. How could he make guys like Jim, or even Walt, understand? They *liked* to run in packs— go out for Little League, Cub Scouts, any noisy bunch they could join. They trooped to shows, to the Rec Center, to the pool in gangs, always shoving and yelling. Sometimes it seemed the more guys they jammed together, the louder they hollered, the better time they had.

How would it sound if he told them the truth—that he'd rather spend hours alone, sitting so still on Knob Hill he could watch field mice scratch their big ears within six inches of him? Or moving so quietly along the creek that bullfrogs and water spiders took off from his shadow?

Jim tightened his hold. "Give! What's your real reason for disappearing every summer? Come to think of it, every day after school, too."

"I don't disappear!"

"Sure you do." Walt studied him curiously. "You scared of sports or something? The way you played softball in gym, I thought—"

"Not scared either!" Dev ducked, twisted, and was free of Jim's grip, though his scalp burned. "Got better things to do."

"Such as?" Jim swiped a long arm toward him, but Walt turned away. In disgust, he spit in the dust. Dev saw the spit leave a dark crater on the ground at his feet, and hated himself for noticing such little things.

"C'mon," Walt growled. "We'll be late for practice. Dev wouldn't help the team anyway if he doesn't want to play. He's just an oddball."

Dev took off again in a sprint, but Walt's last words hung on his back. An oddball. Sure, he was an oddball. He'd seen that plainer and plainer this last year, watching every other guy in the room go out for everything—band, orchestra, stamp club, even patrol last month so next fall they could be big shots and play more yelling games in patrol gym.

Something must really be wrong with him, not wanting to join the crowd the way they did. Maybe it was part of his stupid dumbness. The thought of that report card crammed in his back pocket slowed Dev. His final grades were so bad, mostly D's, the nosy teacher had written on the back, "Devlin could use extra help during summer vacation." What did *she* know about it? Truth was, he was too dumb to get any school stuff ever. And too odd to be anything but a hermit when he grew up. A hermit. Now that was the life. Deep in pine woods, heating a can of beans over a crackling applewood fire . . .

Beans reminded Dev how hard his stomach was chopping. He shot for home. Nikki was already in the kitchen, pretending to loop her long blonde hair over one eye, but actually peeking to see Mom light up at her report card. That was really going to help. Why couldn't Nik be off somewhere baby-sitting?

"All A's!" Mom smiled, and a streak of flour by her mouth curved her smile lopsided. "Nikki, that's wonderful! Let's see yours, son."

Dev tossed it on the counter, glared at Nik—what he could see of her behind that crazy hair—scooped up some cookies, and made for the screen door. With luck, he could be two houses away before Mom got a good look.

Luck wasn't with him.

"Dev!" she cried out.

Dad came running from the living room. "What's wrong?"

Dev slumped against the screen. Now he was in for it. Anybody else's father would still be at work. His father had to be a famous radio announcer, with crazy hours that brought him in on home fights before the word-dust settled. Dev hunched his shoulders and waited, forehead pressed against the screen.

Like Mom, Dad sucked in his breath. What made parents take report cards—his anyway—as if they'd been hit in the stomach? And what made half of him stand off and notice how they acted, even when he was drowning in his own hot water? More of his queerness, probably.

Dad's carefully controlled radio voice was rising, ". . . and your highest grades are C's—in art and gym!"

"I liked those units. We were outdoors most of the time."

"And still you got only C's!"

"Well, C is average."

"AVERAGE!" Dad exploded. "My only son has to be better than average!"

Dev squirmed. That "only son" stuff again.

"Now, Bruce," Mom said, and Dad calmed down a little, the way he always did when Mom "now Bruce'd" him in her quiet voice. But that didn't stop him from delivering a long lecture on how Dev was capable of doing far better than average work—they knew from tests taken in school—how no son of his was going to enter sixth grade with a record so poor, still saying "tooken" for "taken," still not aware that eight eights are sixty-four, still mixing history with literature to invent a writer named Ethan Allen Poe—

"Or thinking George Ham Lincoln was our first president," Nikki giggled.

Dev whirled. "That was in first grade!"

"So what?" Nikki grinned. "Since then, Mr. History-Maker, you've also told us about Kid Carson, Wild Bill Hiccup, and Custard's Last Stand. I ask you!" She leaned against the counter for support against a fit of giggles. "Was that a good place to get a milk shake?"

"Nikki!" This time Mom didn't smile. She exchanged anxious looks with Dad. "I'd forgotten Dev used so many wrong names. Do you suppose he doesn't hear well?"

"He hears perfectly well—when he wants to." Dad scowled. "He has no trouble hearing Mrs. Thornton tap her cane on the porch next door."

"But that's how she calls me to do a job for her! I get money for that."

"You'd get more money if you paid attention to your studies."

Dev stared at his father. What did he mean? Dad never paid a cent for grades, the way some fathers did. Jim boasted his dad gave a dollar for every A, and fifty cents for B's.

"Why glare at me?" Dad thumped the card. "You created this mess—despite all the help we gave you on homework."

"Now, Bruce," Mom said again.

Dev said nothing. No use bringing up the pay-for-grades idea. On that system, they'd have a right to fine him. But what did Dad mean—more money if he paid attention? He'd better not ask, though. That was just what Dad seemed to want—a big chummy father-and-son exchange. Only with Dad, it would be more father-*to*-son. Togetherness with Dad meant listening to *him* talk. Probably because Dad earned his living that way, he couldn't stop talking when he came home. Better not ask what he meant, Dev decided.

Dad sighed. "O.K. son, clam up, as usual. I could show you how better grades mean better schooling. And better schooling means a chance, in the long run, for a better job. My only son must have that chance. But you aren't ready to listen yet. All you can grasp now is the next step, this summer."

Whatever that step was, it wasn't good. Dev caught the you-won't-like-this-but-take-it tone in Dad's voice His stomach muscles braced against whatever bad medicine was coming.

"I was waiting—hoping—until your report card came." Dad said the words so slowly they seemed to hurt. "This record, plus your teacher's note, settles it. You'll have to go to summer school."

"And have all my free time wasted?"

"It better NOT be wasted!"

"Bruce, *please*." Mom pitched her warning higher. "It's only three hours in the morning, son."

"But morning's the best time to be out! And half my chances to work for Mrs. Thornton will be ruined!"

"That's what I meant," Dad said, "about the rewards of paying attention. If your grades were better, you could have earned more this summer. As it is now, you have no choice."

Dev drew a deep, sick breath. Suddenly, he heard himself shouting. "It's not fair. It's not! I'll never be smart like Nikki! I'm dumb. Dumb! Summer school's not going to help me one bit!"

He turned, banged open the screen door without seeing it, and plunged into the hot afternoon. He had to get out, away, to run free. Until today, school was the worst prison. Now home was shutting in, too. Everything, everywhere, was pushing at him. Where could he run to escape?

chapter II

Fire in the Night

"Dev-lin!" Twice, in time with his name, Mrs. Thornton rapped her heavy gold-headed cane on the porch next door. "Come here, please. I need you."

Dev skidded to a stop. In five minutes, he could be halfway up Knob Hill, but her call usually meant a job. A job meant money . . . and this summer he couldn't skip one chance.

Dev took the brick walk slowly. It always seemed funny to him that a grown person could be no bigger than Mrs. Rose Thornton. Although she wore her white hair fluffed high on top of her head and held herself straight as a poplar, still, when he climbed to porch level with her, her brown eyes twinkled barely two inches above his. The odd, quick way she moved, the queer things she said, the sharing way she talked to her dog, all made her seem more like a child than an old lady. An oddball child, Dev thought. Like me. Only in her, the queerness didn't seem stupid.

He made himself smile. "Want me to walk Boon?"

"How did you guess? But I haven't let him out yet. Do you think the night air is too cool?"

Dev glanced at the sun. Two hours, easy, till sunset, and it was sticky hot. But if Mrs. Thornton called this cool night air, so what? He was sick of people telling other people they were wrong, they had to face facts. Maybe, for her, the facts were different. Might as well humor her. He held up a finger. "No wind. It can't be too cool."

"I shouldn't want Boon to catch cold. After all, he is my Boon Companion."

At her double use of his name, Boon reared up tall and laughing and scratched at the screen. He was a very mixed-breed dog, a tricolor, with setter-red head and haunches, the part-white, graceful plumed tail of collie ancestors, the dark, curly body fur of his spaniel mother. Boon would have been warm enough in below-zero weather, but Mrs. Thornton liked to fuss over him.

"Why don't you put on his blanket?" Dev asked. "I'll see he doesn't lose it."

"Perfect!" Mrs. Thornton clapped her tiny hands. "You are 'one of the people on whom nothing is lost.' Henry James."

Dev blinked. "Huh?"

"Henry James. He said: 'Try to be one of the people on whom nothing is lost.' And you are!"

Dev laughed. With school still going, Mrs. Thornton hadn't called him for many errands. He had almost forgotten that part of her queerness—talking about dead writers as if they were still alive, and close friends. Then he remembered her words and laughed harder.

She raised bristly eyebrows. "I see nothing funny in James."

"Oh, he isn't. I mean, it's just that my family wouldn't agree."

"Why not?"

"Well—" Dev could kick himself for opening up that much. It never paid to let a grown-up know what you were thinking. Once they found out, they jumped down your throat. Only maybe Mrs. Thornton wouldn't. She didn't talk the way other people did. He decided to risk it.

"You see, we had sort of—well—a discussion just now. I guess I'm one of the people *everything* gets lost on. My grades are lousy. Dad's socked me into summer school."

Forgetting Boon, Mrs. Thornton plunked into a rocker. "You don't like that?"

"Gee whiz, would you? All your free time tooken away just to rot in some stuffy class?" Dev let his eyes climb Knob Hill, to the top. He pictured the orchard just over the brow. "I had my whole summer planned, too. Mornings up there—" he nodded, "building the best fort yet. Afternoons taking bike hikes with Boon. And now they've wrecked everything!"

He kicked the porch pillar with his sneaker. A few rotting splinters broke off. Hastily, he shoved them in the bushes.

Mrs. Thornton didn't notice. She rocked back and forth, punching her cane into the porch rail with every forward tilt. "Your friends, are they disappointed?"

"Friends?"

"The ones to help you build that fort."

"I haven't got any friends—not people friends anyway."

She brought both feet smack on the floor. "Surely, Devlin, you have some friends. The boys you play with at school—"

"Them?" Dev ran his hand over his scalp. It still hurt from Jim's yanks this afternoon. He thought about Walt, looking blue and dumpy like an eggplant in his Cub Scout uniform. Walt never bullied, but he always had to have a pack of kids around to be happy. "They're all right," Dev lied. "I'd just rather be alone."

Mrs. Thornton chuckled. " 'I never found the companion that was so companionable as solitude.' Thoreau."

He tried to be polite. "Who?"

"A friend of mine." Her eyes clouded. "Dev, you remind me of my son Roger. Of course, he's much older than you—a grown man now—with important things to lure him away. But when he was your age, he always wore a little frown, like you. And he always seemed to be taking in more than he gave out—just like you."

Dev felt a stir of excitement. If somebody else was like him, then maybe he wasn't so different after all. "What's Roger doing now?"

"Just—wandering." Mrs. Thorton sighed, and drew her sweater closer about her narrow shoulders. "He always wandered, even as a child. The times I've waited supper for him!"

Supper. Dev glanced at his house. Almost time for Mom to call. But if he could be out of sight and not hear her, be off on an errand for Mrs. T, he wouldn't have to be home on time. Or at all. He still had five cookies in his pocket. Maybe that's why Boon scratched so hard at the screen.

"Mrs. Thornton, if you'll get Boon's blanket—"

"Oh, how could I forget my treasure?" She hurried inside. After buckling the dog into a thick green blanket covered with crocheted pink roses, she let him escape. Boon streaked from porch to front walk before Dev caught his leash.

"Be a good dog, dear," Mrs. Thornton called. "Don't catch cold!"

Dev ran Boon around the far side of Mrs. Thornton's house, past the bay window, through the back hedge. Behind lay Walt's house, but Walt probably wasn't finished with Little League yet.

Only he was. In the garage, Jim and Walt bent together

over Walt's green go-cart. They were lettering "The W-J Jet" on its side in black paint.

Boon stopped to investigate. Walt looked up and grinned.

"Hey, Dev. Join the fun!"

"Can't. Got to walk Boon."

"Call that a walk?" Jim spattered his paintbrush at Boon. Dev jerked the dog out of range, and Boon choked.

"Boy, wait'll I tell old lady Thornpuss how you handle that beast," Jim jeered. "She'll turn you in for cruelty to dumb animals!"

With trembling hands, Dev checked the blanket to be sure it had escaped the paint, then snatched it off. Jim probably wouldn't say anything, but if Mrs. T found out, she'd be mad. Maybe if he got Jim to arguing, he'd forget. "Boon's not a dumb beast!"

"Maybe not compared to you."

Walt straightened up. "Knock it off, Jim. Listen, Dev, stick around for once. Let this dry a few minutes, and we'll give Boon the ride of his life."

Dev shook his head. "He's supposed to be running, not riding."

Jim tapped his forehead. "No brains. No sporting blood, neither."

Down the block a cat crossed the street, and Boon charged. Dev took off after him, glad for the need to keep up. Anything to get away from those two. The shortest tangle with them meant trouble. It was better not to talk to people at all, ever. Today was a perfect example. Dad lectured. Mrs. Thornton pried. And Jim stabbed, whether he used sharp fingers or sharper words. Even Walt, maybe O.K. by himself, kept trying to shove him into fun and games with other kids.

No sir. For Oddball Dev Bates, playing or talking with other people was no good. The best time of all was time alone with Boon.

Panting together, boy and dog raced past the newer homes in the suburb, past houses with lawns still ungraded, up the bulldozed slopes where the next narrow lots were already staked out.

Mrs. T had been crazy to sell this land, Dev thought. Once she'd owned every inch of it—trees, fields, hill, creek. Then she sold all except the lot her house was on and the very tip top of Knob Hill to a builder. Trees fell. Fields were scraped bare. And the last patch of country was pushed back to the foot of Knob Hill. Soon even that would be broken out into yellow clay mounds, raw houses, and yapping people, with more yapping kids.

If Mrs. T had just held on to more of her land. But maybe she had to sell it to get money to live on. With Roger just wandering, he didn't earn a regular salary the way Dad did.

Dev pushed the thought away because there was the queerness, the wanting to be off by yourself, seeming to be wrong again.

Hurrying up the hill, his sneakered feet welcomed the softer, easier spring of packed earth. He unsnapped Boon's leash. The dog bounded off, snuffling a rabbit trail along the hillside. The blanket hung heavy in Dev's hand, until he fastened it like an Indian game pouch at his belt. Then, more slowly, he climbed to his favorite sitting rock where he could look for miles to the east over the rolling Iowa farmlands, or over suburb and town to the west. He needed time—and quiet —to figure some way out of this summer school mess. If he could.

How good it felt sitting there letting his insides quiet down, while he watched earth settle from day into night.

At first, the farm view spread wide below him to the east, interrupted by neatly spaced orchards and shiny patches of oak and walnut woods. With the sun slanting low, he could make out cattle dotting square fields, and piglets bouncing in long humpy lines after sows.

Then, after the sun burned down behind a dull tan layer of dust, he turned toward town and watched dark creep in slow and narrow, like a cat sneaking up on a mouse, hardly seeming to move at all, and then pounce, it was night! Black night, with heat lightning flickering low to the west, just above the pink neon cloud that kept everyone in town from seeing the few stars popping out.

Boon panted back several times, throwing himself down to rest. They shared the last cookie crumbs, and Boon ran off again. Dev could hear his dog tags clinking. Boon was good for hours of exploring. Dev sat with his knees pulled up to his chin.

Why couldn't he figure some easy way out of this mess? He should have ditched the report card, hidden it under the bridge, weighted by a rock. Then Dad wouldn't have known.

But he'd have found out somehow. Called the principal, or the teacher, to check up on his priceless only son. If Dad just didn't care so much. Only he did. He wanted his only son to be great so he could boast about him in Rotary Club and Junior Chamber of Commerce and everywhere. Like father, like son. Except this son was a failure.

Dev dug his chin harder into crossed arms. What a trap growing up was! People always said it was so wonderful, so nice to be young. Nuts! Either they lied, or they forgot. All those years of school ahead, all that smother of Don'ts and Musts and Let's-Try-Harder, Shall We? With home ninety times worse than school. Instead of one teacher yapping at thirty kids, two parents yelled at two. Nope, one. Dad and Mom never bothered Nikki. She always did what they wanted. She had it easy!

The low whine of a fire siren made Dev lift his head. Half a mile toward town, red lights flashed. The whine climbed to a wail. It was heading this way! Dev scanned the suburb. He saw flame on his block—no, the next one nearest. It looked like Walt's garage was on fire!

Dev jumped up. He whistled for Boon, then called, "Here, Boon! Boon!"

No dog came. Dev whistled louder, started down the hill. Boon's blanket thumped warm and heavy against his leg. The dog wasn't to be seen. Dev combed the hillside, whistling— half watching the fire, but more worried about the dog. It couldn't have been a big fire. The one engine left soon.

Where was that dog? Maybe he'd gone home by himself. After a few more piercing whistles, and a hasty, anxious climb to the other side of the hill, Dev knew he had to face Mrs. Thornton.

He angled down the slope, back the long blocks, whistling so hard his lips dried and ached by the time he reached Walt's.

Jim popped from the shadows. "Where you been? Every-body's been looking for you. You missed a dandy fire!"

"Who's everybody?"

"Your folks. Mrs. Thornton. The police. Where you been?"

The police! Uneasily, Dev said, "Looking for Boon. He ran off somewhere. Have you seen him?"

"Not that beast. You shoulda been here. Flames shot half-way up the wall! And the W-J Jet is ruined."

Dev glanced in the garage. Except for the hulk of the go-cart and a dark patch of blistered paint, he couldn't see that much had happened. "What started it?"

"You mean *who* started it." Jim was so excited he couldn't stand still. He kept circling the go-cart. "Me and Walt picked up the paint rags and hung 'em on that trash can before we went in the house for some lemonade. And then we got interested in a TV program and were laughing like crazy, when all of a sudden Walt smells smoke. We rush out, and you know what? Somebody'd stuffed those paint rags under the go-cart! They were going up like the Fourth of July!"

"Maybe you just thought you picked up the rags—"

Jim stopped prowling. "Say, what're you trying to do, blame us? We hung the rags up, I tell you. Somebody else moved them." His eyes narrowed, took on a mean look. "Maybe you did."

"What would I do a dumb thing like that for?"

"I don't know. Because you're dumb, maybe, or mad at me for teasing you." Jim spoke so slowly he seemed to be think-ing out loud. "You had plenty of chance. All that time your folks said you were missing, maybe you hid in the bushes, just watching for us to go in."

"Well, I didn't! I was—" Dev stopped. Why tell Jim any-thing about the sitting rock? He would plant himself up there and ruin it. "I told you, looking for Boon."

"Yeah? Tell that to the police." Jim grinned.

"Why the police?"

"Because me and Walt told them about the paint rags being moved, and they wrote it all down. And your folks told them they were worried cause you hadn't been home for hours. It's gonna look awful funny for you, kid."

"You're nuts!" Dev ran from the garage. He wanted to tear straight home, past his waiting family if he could, and up to his bedroom. But first he had to check with Mrs. Thornton. He brushed through the hedge, ran around the house and up the front steps. If Boon would just come barking! The heavy wooden door behind the screen was shut. He twisted the old-fashioned doorbell.

Mrs. Thornton opened the door a crack. "There you are!" She sounded breathless. "Boon came back twenty minutes ago, so dirty I had to shut him down cellar. He's lost his leash and blanket, too."

"No, he hasn't." Dev was so relieved he didn't care if Mrs. T scolded him for an hour. He unsnapped the blanket from his belt, handed her the leash through the crack. "Boon ran so hard on the hill he didn't need that cover."

She opened the door wider. "So that's where you were. You had everybody worried, sure you'd run off."

Dev laughed. "I wouldn't take Boon with me if I did."

"I should hope not. I'd hate to lose him and the blanket, too."

"I didn't lose the blanket." Dev started to explain again, but she stopped him.

"What were you doing up there? You can't build forts in the dark."

"Just—thinking, I guess."

"Hmph! I hired you to walk Boon. Instead, you were thinking. 'To do two things at once is to do neither.' Publilius Syrus."

There she went again. Dev started off the porch. "You don't have to pay me."

"Come back!" She opened the screen. Under the porch light, one coin shone in her outstretched hand. "You not only walked Boon, you ran him. I should pay you twice as much, because he needs exercise. But I do not believe in rewarding neglect of duty. You weren't exactly careful. Take just this dime. Take it!"

Her tone was so commanding, Dev obeyed. "Well, thank you, Mrs. Thornton. I'll be more careful next time—if you'll trust me."

"I'll trust you. 'The biggest dog has been a pup.' Joaquin Miller," she snapped, and shut the door.

Pup! Boy, she really was crazy. Boon was at least three years old. Dev shrugged and slid the dime in his pocket. He'd better streak for home.

One foot inside the kitchen, and they hit.

"It's Dev!" Nikki screeched.

"Where have you been?" Mom rustled to meet him. "We've been so worried! You didn't even come home for supper."

"Mrs. Thornton asked me to run Boon."

"For five hours?" Dad held the paper before him, but he wasn't reading it. It was crumpled and shook in his hands.

"Boon got away. I had to look for him. And before that, I was just sitting."

"Where?" Dad demanded.

"I told you. Up on the hill."

"No, you didn't tell me." Dad's tone was icy. "And how could you see to sit or to run Boon up there? There are no lights on that hill."

In silence, Dev faced his father. Hadn't he ever been out at night? Or had he lived so long walled in by the city, moving from house lights to street lights to fluorescent tubes in sound-proof rooms at the radio station that he'd dimmed the use of his eyes and ears in the night? Didn't he know you could see plenty by stars or cloud reflections? And track by sounds? For once Dev opened his mouth to answer his father, and then he remembered. Up in that half-darkness he had lost Boon. He hadn't managed to watch the dog, any more than he'd seen a way out of summer school. In defeat, he swallowed the answer he could have made.

His father stood up. "You know there was a fire tonight?"

"Yes, I saw it—from the hill!"

"That may be. You were missing during the hours that fire started. The last persons to see you were Walt and Jim, who teased you, and whose go-cart was destroyed. And we had to tell the police you were gone. Was anyone with you on the hill? Any—witness?" For a second Dad sounded hopeful.

"I told you. I went there with Boon! Why won't you believe me?"

"Son, I want to believe you! I do believe you, except—"

Except. That meant he really didn't. Dev turned for the stairs before the rest of the lecture could spout, but Dad said, "Wait!" Dev waited without turning around. He could hear the grayness, the tiredness in Dad's voice.

"You must learn to look at these things the way other people see them. It's difficult to believe that a boy your age who can't sit still one hour of daytime in school would have the will and the courage to sit still so many hours in the dark. Can't you see how peculiar it seems?"

Peculiar! Dev winced. "Can I go now?"

"In a moment. It's certainly true that Boon came back alone. That fits with the rest of your story, but it also means you did not carry out your job responsibly. Dev, you have so much to learn!"

"May I go to my room now?"

"Don't you want any supper?" Mom asked. "I saved you some."

"Or I'll fix you a sandwich," Nikki offered.

"I don't want anything." Very quietly, so he wouldn't be called back for stamping, Dev went upstairs. Very quietly, he shut the door to his room. He went straight to the toy pirate chest that held his savings. He spilled all the coins on his bed: 50¢, $1.50, $2.75, with tonight's dime, $2.85. Fifteen cents more, and he'd have three dollars. Not near enough. But boy, would he learn. Only not the way Dad expected.

The whole year through, he'd learn to save his money. By next summer, he'd have enough to take off. Outdoors, all the time. Away from school. Away from people who wanted you to talk, and then wouldn't believe what you said. Away from crazy kids who got you in trouble no matter what you did or didn't do.

What was it Mrs. Thornton said tonight? Something about doing two things at once didn't work? Well, he'd keep his mind on just one thing. Saving money.

To make sure, he hauled out an old looseleaf notebook, turned to the middle of clean pages, and in his best writing, put down:

"I, Devlin Bates, will learn to ern my own way."

He looked critically at the words. Something was wrong with "ern." He blew dust from his dictionary, flipped to the E's. After some searching, he found the correct spelling, and added the missing a.

Still, he wasn't satisfied. The vow needed some strong reason for it. After all, going away from home, even with money saved up, was an awful big step.

He nibbled a thumbnail to help him think. Then he knew what to add.

"I will give Them egzactly one year to change—or else!"

Restricted

"Devlin! This is my last call!"

"I'm up," he yelled. He put both feet on the floor to make it half true. Early mornings last summer had been so good to run out in—when the grass squashed wet underfoot and the zigzag stitch on the garden spider's web hung beaded with mist. Now the same mornings were ruined. What fun could you have any summer day spoiled by three drippy hours of school? Better to stay in bed and stall it off as long as possible.

"Devlin! I don't hear you walking around!"

Without rising, he stamped his feet several times, one after the other, on the hooked rug.

"Faker." Nikki poked her head around the door. "You better get up. Mrs. T wants you to mail a letter before school."

"Then get out!" Dev heaved a pillow at her.

"Missed me!" Nikki giggled and disappeared.

Dev snatched blue jeans from beneath a chair. In two minutes sharp, bruised by a closet door knob but wakened by hurrying, he was dressed, face splashed with water, hair slicked with one pass of the brush, and downstairs. "Where's the letter?"

"Mrs. Thornton said after breakfast was time enough." Mom fastened his top shirt button.

He wrenched it open. "That's too tight!"

She fastened it again and smoothed his collar. "Leave it alone. You're growing, but not that much. What are you hunting for?"

"Matches." Dev found and pocketed a bunch. "Marshmallows, too. I want to cook some at my fort after school."

His mother tucked a few in a sandwich bag. Dev counted them. "Five! That's not near enough!"

Dad glanced up hopefully from his paper. "Got a gang to join you?"

Dev hesitated. He could lie, but his father might check up. Dad often had some daytime hours free. It would be just like him to "take a stroll" and just "happen" to pass the fort Dev had been able to build in his few spare hours.

"Just a gang of nuthatches," Dev said.

Dad muttered something about "for the birds."

Mom sighed. She handed Dev the five marshmallows. "This is plenty then."

In silence, so he could eat faster, Dev crammed sweet roll, banana, cereal, and milk. Then he grabbed his homework and dashed out the kitchen door. He didn't bother to say good-bye. Dad could make him sit through summer school, but he couldn't make him like it. Not saying good-bye was one more way to show him what he thought.

Outdoors, he yanked his collar open. He found Mrs. T kneeling in her backyard, beside the slanted cellar door. She was weeding. Boon, stretched beneath a lilac bush, thumped his tail when Dev approached, but Mrs. Thornton didn't look up.

Dev coughed. "You're out early!"

She jumped, then smiled up at him, blinking her eyes against the sun. "I've always agreed," she said, "with R.L.S. 'Though we should be grateful for good houses, there is, after all, no house like God's out-of-doors.' R.L.S. is Robert Louis Stevenson, you know." She attacked another bunch of weeds so hard she nearly lost her balance.

Dev struggled to hide a smile. For someone who liked the outdoors, she sure treated it rough. "I could do that for you this afternoon."

She shook her head. "You work too much for me already, Devlin. You should play more. Besides, I like to pull weeds. Cast out the useless!"

Dev shifted his feet. "Uh—didn't you want me to mail a letter?"

"Indeed, I did. I do. Oh, I'm so forgetful!" She peeled off the white canvas gloves she always wore for gardening and got up stiffly. "I particularly want this to reach Roger in time. June thirtieth is his birthday."

"But this is—" Dev chopped off the rest. Today was July first. He had turned the calendar in his room last night. Mrs. T didn't realize it. Should he tell her? That would be dumb. It wouldn't change the date and would only make her unhappy. He decided to keep still.

Too late. She had cocked her head like a curious brown sparrow. "This is what?"

"Oh—just a nice day to—to go to the mailbox."

"You're right!" She swept her cane in a vigorous arc which took in the whole summer day. " 'There is no season such

delight can bring, as summer, autumn, winter, and the spring.'
William Browne!"

"The letter, Mrs. Thornton?"

She clapped tiny hand to mouth, then hurried into the
house and returned, bringing an envelope. She pressed the
usual dime on Dev. "Thank you, my dear. I don't know what
I should do without you!"

"Yes'm." Dev rode his bike as fast as he could to the mailbox, then slowly toward school. The school, built new to take
care of kids in this end of town, wasn't a bad-looking place.
But just two summers before killdeers had nested where the
school stood now. Once Dev had seen one big striped mother
bird run ahead, pretending her wing was broken and dragging
it in the dust to draw him farther from her nest. All the time,
the male circled overhead, crying, "Kill-dee! Kill-dee!" No
pair nested here this year. The plowed earth they'd liked was
hardpacked playground now, and all the killdeers had retreated farther into the country. That was reason enough to
hate school—as if there weren't twenty others.

Halfway to school, he passed Walt and Jim. They were
swiping at hedges with a butterfly net. Dev braked and
slowed. "Where'd you get the net?"

"It's an old one of my Dad's." Walt swung it suddenly,
then peered inside. "Nuts! Lost it!"

"You have to swing easier for butterflies," Dev said.

"Who said anything about flutterbys?" Jim sneered. "We're
trapping bees."

"What for?"

"Because we hate them. All they do is sting!"

"They help fertilize crops—" Dev began.

"How would you know, dummy? Go on to summer school.

C'mon, Walt. Gimme the net. I'll catch a jillion, and we'll drown 'em in kerosene!"

Dev rode off, pedaling furiously. One year. One year would never change them, but he wouldn't have to stick around and watch them kill bees again, either.

All morning, class dragged. There were only ten from town in fifth grade review. Mrs. Vogel, the teacher, wore glasses, and spoke in a husky voice. Usually she was patient and smiling. Today they were reviewing states across America—old stuff, boring as last year. Dev found it impossible to sit still. He twisted to stare out the open windows, past flies so stupid they climbed the shut glass. They wanted to escape into the hot bright day and couldn't see how to get out. Any more than I can, Dev thought.

"Devlin," Mrs. Vogel said, "what is Iowa noted for?"

"Corn," Dev answered easily, remembering the knee-high fields he could see from his fort. "And pigs." Then he thought about a report on one of Dad's newscasts about hundreds of turkeys killed by flocking together in a heat wave. When he'd asked about them, Dad said they were just a small part of thousands in a farmer's flock. "Turkeys, too. Iowa raises lots of turkeys."

"*Very* good! Now what state borders Iowa to the west?"

Dev stared at the blackboard. West—he'd never traveled that way. Dad always combined their vacation with some convention in the East. Dev tried to recall the geography map. Beyond Iowa, until California, it flowed into a yellow, orange blank.

"Nebraska borders Iowa to the west," some girl behind him said, and Mrs. Vogel gave a pleased nod.

Dev settled back to dreaming. He wouldn't be called on for another five minutes if he was lucky.

After school Dev beat it for the fort. Leaning his bike against a tree before the hill turned steep, he approached the site stealthily. He'd named it Fort Rabies, in honor of Boon's discarded rabies tag rescued from the trash and hung on an apple limb shading the fort.

Fort Rabies lay in a hollow, just over the east brow of the hill. Completely hidden from the suburb, it was safe enough from spying because not many kids messed around up here. Still, with school out, Dev couldn't be sure. Once he'd found all the branches that he'd fitted together for the fort knocked down. It had taken him a whole Saturday morning to build them up again.

Today, nothing was bothered. No one had been here. The brass tag glinted as it twisted in the light breeze. The laced branches stood, leaning slightly north, but strong enough. Dev paused to admire his doorway. He had found one smooth curving log. By propping it high between two tall forked up-right limbs, he had built an arched doorway for his one room fort. He always stepped through this door with a feeling of coming home.

But today when he entered, he stopped quickly. He had almost stumbled into a bed of coals! They were cold he discovered, by spitting on them, but someone *had* been here. Last night, probably, because the coals hadn't been here when he left about four yesterday afternoon.

Dev searched inside the fort. Sunlight filtered through the branches. He could see every twig. Nothing else was burned, no branches were broken off. Whoever it was must have dragged wood in here from his pile outside. On the board shelf in one corner, his carton of fossils and the two blue jay feathers lay untouched. Kids usually knocked over or took what they found. What if the visitor was a tramp? Dev felt a prickle of fear and pride. His fort would make a perfect place for a tramp to spend the night!

But when he looked again, he saw the fire had been exactly centered, so it left too little room inside for sleeping. Who could have been here? Dev hunted outside for more clues. Nothing. Whoever had prowled around here probably just wanted a fire for fun. Anyway, it made a dandy bed for a marshmallow fire.

Dev raked the coals together with his hands and added twigs and larger sticks till he had a teepee-shaped mound of wood. The wood was so dry it caught with one match. The fire gave off that wonderful smell of applewood smoke.

Too hungry for the first marshmallow, Dev cooked it in leaping flames. It came out pure burnt sugar. Dev threw it to the ants. The second marshmallow puffed and blistered to a golden brown, and he ate it, content.

The birds had dropped into their noon hush. It was so still Dev could hear the click and whir of a grasshopper jumping outside. He liked the absence of voices, the hardness of earth beneath him—so different from the hardness of cement. What did Walt and Jim, running around trapping bees, know about squatting down and just watching and listening to what happened around them? Even if they did get better grades . . .

From town, the one o'clock whistle blared. Dev knew he'd better get home quick for lunch, or Mom would be hopping mad.

He poked the fire apart with a stick, then kicked dust over it. After a last check around Fort Rabies, he went back to his bike and, once on the level, mounted it and zoomed. Nothing worth taking time to see down here, anyway.

At home, he remembered to wash his hands. It might keep

Mom from getting mad at him for being late. Nikki followed him into the bathroom. She emerged at once with a shriek.

"Mother! He left the soap so dirty I have to wash it before I can wash my hands!"

Mother clucked her tongue. "Now, Nikki, you're exaggerating."

"Am I?" Nikki scooped up the soap on a washcloth and waved it under Mom's nose. "Look at it!"

Mom backed up to see better. "It's dirty all right. What do you do up there, Dev?"

"Somebody started a fire," Dev said.

"Did you have to put it out with your bare hands?" Nikki asked. "Why don't you join Scouts, the way Dad wants you to, and learn their eleventh law? 'A Scout is Clean.' "

"Aw, Scouts are too noisy," Dev said. "All they do is run around in crowded rooms and holler."

"How do you know?" Nikki said. "You only went once."

"Oh, shut up!"

"Devlin!" Mom opened her mouth to start her most exasperated lecture, when the doorbell chimed. She settled for a scolding glance and went to answer.

Dev heard a man's deep voice. Then Mom opened the door and a policeman came in. His blue uniform seemed to fill the living room.

"Sorry to bother you, Mrs. Bates. We're doing some checking around the neighborhood and thought your son might be able to help us. Is he here?"

"Devlin?" Mom backed up. "Yes, of course. I'm sure he'll be glad to help you."

Dev rose from the couch. All policemen made him nervous —even the quiet one who'd talked to him the day after the fire at Seldings' and who'd seemed to believe Dev was telling the truth. But this was a different man, much younger, with a stern no-nonsense mouth.

"You're Devlin Bates?"

"Yes." That was easy.

"How often do you play up on Knob Hill?"

"Why—almost every day." Dev stared at the man. What was wrong with playing there? It wasn't fenced, or posted with "Keep Off" signs.

"Ever take matches up there?"

"Yes. I did today," Dev said slowly. "But I just lit a little fire to toast marshmallows!"

The policeman looked at him closely. "What did you use for kindling?"

"The old dead limbs from those trees the bulldozers pushed down. What's wrong with that? It's just rotting up there. And I put out the fire before I left!"

"We know that, son. We checked, when we got a report of smoke over that hilltop."

"Shouldn't Dev play up there?" Mom asked nervously. "We've tried to train him to be careful with fire."

"He probably is." The man seemed to be weighing his next words. "But somebody around here isn't. We found a stack of scrap lumber burning at one of the new homesites early this morning."

"Don't the workmen start those fires?" Nikki hated to be left out of anything.

"Not this one. We checked. They said the pile wasn't big enough yet." The policeman hesitated. "Maybe it doesn't mean a thing. But two unexplained fires in this neighborhood in less than a month looks suspicious. Could be just children

playing around—or we could have a firebug on our hands."
Was he looking at Dev for a warning?

"I haven't started any fires!" Dev protested. "Except at my
fort, and that was just to toast marshmallows." He felt silly,
saying the same thing over again.

"Well, maybe you shouldn't take matches up on the hill for
a while," the policeman said. "And if you see anything suspicious, let us know, will you? You boys have a way of getting
around."

"Sure." Dev was relieved to see the man head for the door.
Maybe he took the answers for truth—and maybe he didn't.

Mom hurried back from seeing him out. "Are you telling
the truth, Dev? The honest truth?"

"Of course I am! Cross my heart! I haven't set any fires!"

But she didn't let it rest at that. When Dad came home for
supper, Mom told him about the policeman's call and how
he'd asked especially for Dev.

Dad scowled. "Son, you did take matches up on the hill this
morning."

"Only for marshmallows." Silently, Dev promised himself
he'd never cook another one.

"I'm sure it's just coincidence, and perfectly innocent on
your part," Dad said, "the matches this morning, and your
absence when Seldings' garage caught fire. But I cannot have
my only son suspected of setting fires. For your own safety,
Dev, I'm going to ask that you stay in this house and yard
until further notice."

Dev stared. Then he whooped. "No more summer school?"

"Summer school goes on, of course!" Dad said. "But you
must come directly home afterwards. No playing at your fort.
No wandering alone in the afternoon."

"What about working for Mrs. Thornton? If I stay here, I can't do that!"

Dad glanced at Mom. Her return glance seemed to plead with him. "Well, if you stay in sight of the house, I guess you can't get in much mischief."

"I haven't *been* in any mischief!"

"Probably you haven't, son. But I want to make sure."

The way he said it made Dev sick. His father didn't trust him! He thought his only son wasn't just dumb, but a criminal. And Mom wasn't much better. It was enough to make you want to do something crazy, just because they thought you were doing it anyway!

"Dad?" Nikki asked.

"Well?" The one word dared her to speak.

She glanced at Dev, as if afraid to say anything, yet afraid to keep still. "When Dev came home today, *before* the policeman was here, he said somebody had set a fire."

"That's right! They did!" Dev suddenly remembered. "Last night, somebody built a fire inside my fort! The coals were cold on the ground when I got there!"

Dad looked suddenly relieved. "Did you tell the policeman that?"

"No, I forgot. But it's true."

His father leaned forward. "Can you show the police where that fire was built?"

"Sure, I—" Dev stopped. He had built his fire on top of the other. The police, when they checked up there, had seen the remains of just one.

He saw Dad close his eyes. When he opened them, they brimmed with such a mixture of anger and shame Dev had to look away. "Don't," his father said. "Don't add lying to your other weaknesses. Please!"

Dev tore upstairs. Every last thing he said and did turned against him! He couldn't win! And *they* weren't changing. They were getting worse. The only thing to do was get out from under.

He counted his growing pile of money—$8.50. Dad's rule, making him stay near the house, still left him free to work for Mrs. Thornton. Slowly, as the money came in, it was insurance he could go. For every charge his parents made against him, every complaint, he'd go one state farther west. That was the way he'd travel.

Dumbness. The next state west of Iowa was Nebraska.

Suspicion of setting fires. What was next beyond Nebraska? He ripped his geography from the shelf. Wyoming if he went north, Colorado if he went south. Wyoming looked wilder— not so many towns. He'd go that way.

What was the next charge? *Lying.* The next state west of Wyoming was Idaho. That meant he was already three counts and three states away.

He looked at the $8.50 again. So little! But with hitch-hiking, and as much food as he could take from home, he could stretch it through Nebraska at least. He'd have a lot more than $8.50 saved when the year was up, anyway. Early June was farming time, so out West he'd have no trouble getting a job. Idaho would have lots of potatoes to plant, and then dig. He'd find some place way back off the main roads —a place where no one would ever think to look for him. And if you built a fire, it was O.K. because you were only trying to cook your own food.

chapter IV

Shadow's Picnic

Dev didn't really like cats. They killed too many birds. But he had to admit Nikki's new kitten, Shadow, wasn't bad.

Shadow turned up on the morning newspaper one cool Sunday in August. Half-grown, yowling with hunger, he crouched in the middle of the *Des Moines Register* and refused to move until Nikki set down a pie pan of milk. Then he ran to it and slopped up every drop, except what he splattered against the porch steps. He looked, as Nikki said, thinner than a shadow. It was hard to tell which stood out plainer—his stripes or his ribs.

Mom argued against keeping such a "sick-looking creature."

"He's not sick—just hungry," Dev said. "All he needs is food and a little time to fill out."

For once, Nikki sided with Dev. She wanted to keep the kitten because he had such a rasping purr. "Like the sewing machine, when I'm trying to put in a zipper." She also pointed out that since Dev was still restricted to the neighborhood and never invited friends in to play, a cat might stop his complaining about not being able to go to the fort.

Mom threw up her hands. "All right! But you'll have to feed him!"

Both Dev and Nikki took this order personally. They each fed Shadow several times a day. He ate everything. His stomach, Dev figured, must have been round and stretchable like a balloon. He grew sleek, shining, and smart enough never to run up the curtains when Mom was in the room.

It was just such a planned trip Shadow gave up one afternoon when Mom came downstairs carrying Indian notepaper.

Dev took one look and groaned. "Not now!"

"Now. This afternoon!" She thumped paper, pen, envelope, and stamp in front of him. "Everything you need is there. When I get back, I want that letter done. The idea of not thanking your grandparents yet for their nice birthday gift!"

"Where you going?" Dev saw she was all dressed up— gloves, hat, heels—not the way she usually looked, even for shopping.

"Oh, just downtown." The way she said it sounded like half the truth. "Nikki, make sure Dev finishes that letter."

"I won't be here," Nikki said. "I'm sitting for the Reeds."

"I forgot." Mom frowned. "Well, if you should need Nikki, you know where to phone, Dev."

"Don't worry. I won't need anybody."

Mom sighed. "That's just the trouble."

With both Mom and Nikki gone, Dev could hear every noise in the house. The refrigerator sang to itself. The clock sounded like high heels clicking on pavement. Shadow's paws drummed on the rug. Dev snapped on the radio, caught his father giving the two o'clock news, and snapped it off quick.

He flipped through the notepaper. Indian faces, from four different tribes. They were supposed to make him *like* writing letters. Well, they didn't. He took the pen and colored a Crow Indian's piercing eyes bright blue. It looked all wrong and pleased Dev somehow.

It was so hard to write "thank you" letters. After he'd written "Thank you. I like the brithday gift you sent very much," what else could he say? And still almost two pages to fill. Even if he scrawled the writing huge, he had to put something more.

Shadow, tired of playing with a marble, yawned and curled up in a patch of sunshine. Now there was something to write about!

"We have a new cat," Dev wrote. "When he yauns, his tung curls up like a ski jump, only it's pink." Pretty soon, just describing Shadow, he'd covered both pages. The letter was finished.

He stamped it, started to address it, but then couldn't remember what Gramp's house number was. Oh well, that could be done later, in seconds.

He pounced on Shadow, rubbing the cat's fur the wrong way. Shadow woke up, said "Prr-rr-up?" and rolled over.

"You deserve a reward for making that old letter easy," Dev told the cat. "I'll fix you the best snack you ever had!"

He carried Shadow to the kitchen and dumped him. The cat purred and arched around Dev's leg, helping him inspect the open refrigerator.

"It ought to be a real picnic, Shad. Everything you like!" Dev took a divided plastic plate, spooned tuna, cottage cheese, and a hunk of liver into one section. He poured milk in the next section. The milk looked kind of thick. Dev smelled it. Ugh! Buttermilk! But maybe Shad would like it anyhow.

Dev dipped his finger in the buttermilk and held it out. Shadow licked off every drop and sat back, yowling for more.

"Hey!" Dev said. "Maybe we've been cheating you, giving you the same stuff all the time." He inspected the refrigerator with new vision. Why not try to change a cat's diet? Maybe he could make a brand-new discovery about what a cat liked.

Dev slid the lid from a bowl. Cookie dough! Well, why not? *He* liked it. He scooped some for himself and put a wad the size of two bubble gum pieces on Shadow's plate. Dev removed another lid. Lemon gelatin. Try that, too. It was all nourishing. That's what Mom kept saying when he didn't want to try something. And ice cream was milk, really, so a spoon of vanilla ice cream hit the plate.

But the choice looked kind of pale. Not enough color. Dev poured catsup on the cottage cheese. There! Shad's picnic-experiment was beginning to look better.

Something was still missing—some last touch Shadow would especially like. Catnip! Mrs. Thornton had some growing in her backyard. Dev had seen a patch when he mowed her lawn, and she'd offered him all he wanted for Shadow. She would be asleep now, taking her afternoon nap, so he shouldn't bother her. But she wouldn't mind if he snitched a few leaves.

"You wait," he told the cat. "Be right back!"

When he returned, waving two stalks of catnip, Shadow had leaped on top of the kitchen counter. He was chewing the liver, his head turned sideways in greed.

"Bad Shad!" Dev swooped him down. "I told you to wait!"

He crushed the catnip by rolling it in his hands. The leaves were so fresh they bruised, and smelled sort of skunky. Shadow yowled louder than ever and butted his head into Dev's shin.

Dev sprinkled the catnip over the entire spread. Perfect! With a courtly flourish, he presented the dish to the cat. Shadow attacked it, and in a few minutes had gobbled half the food.

"You may go down in cat history yet, old boy."

Dev decided it was a good day to wash his bike and set the hose running in the backyard. He had all the dust off and was scouring rust spots from the rear rim when he heard a yell. He looked up. Nikki was back from baby-sitting and was screaming from her bedroom window.

"Dev! Come quick! I think Shadow's dying!"

Dev dropped the hose and ran. He found Shad rolling and heaving on the bedroom floor. His sides turned from valleys to mountains and back to valleys again. His mouth twitched. His green eyes blazed brighter than neon.

Nikki sobbed. "He's having fits!"

"Aw, I bet it's just catnip—maybe."

"What catnip?"

"I gave him some."

"How much?"

"Quite a bit—plus some other stuff."

"He's never acted like that with catnip before." Nikki couldn't take her eyes off Shadow. "What other stuff?"

Shad leaped to his feet. He crouched. His sides convulsed. After three violent heaves and a deep cough, Nikki had the answer spread before her.

"Oooh! You poisoned him!"

"I did not!" Dev yelled. "I just tried a new way of feeding him."

"What on earth is the trouble in here?" Mom, unheard, had come home, too. She peered into the room. "Oh!" She backed out quickly, looking green. "Nikki, you'll have to clean that up. I can't."

"But I didn't do it! Dev poisoned Shadow with what he fed him!"

"What did you feed him?" Mom's voice was awful.

Dev told her.

"Didn't you know he couldn't keep all that down?"

"I'm sorry," Dev said. "I didn't mean to make him sick. I just wanted to see if cats would like what humans do."

"Well, they don't. Honestly, Dev, I don't know why you do such strange things! I wonder if I'll be able to trust you—" She stopped, and shuddered. "Nikki's right. It's your job to clean up. Do it thoroughly!" She almost ran down the hall.

Nikki went out, taking Shad with her. "I'll get the rug cleaner. I don't want my rug ruined!"

It took Dev quite some time. After he finished, he brought the bucket back through the kitchen just in time to hear Nikki reading his letter aloud.

"Mother, get this! 'Shadow's all one color, only his body is grey'—g-r-e-y—'and his stripes are gray'—g-r-a-y. Isn't that crazy?"

"What's crazy?" Dev snatched the letter. "G-r-e-y is light, and g-r-a-y is dark! That's how I see it!"

"You sure see some queer things!"

"Who told you to read my mail, anyway?"

"Stop it!" Mom cried out. She was huddled on the couch and still looked pale. "Dev, may I see your letter?"

He tossed it to her. As she read it, an odd look spread over her face. "Honey, that's—why, that's a *nice* letter. I know they'll be pleased."

"Well, the dumb thing's done, anyhow."

"Not quite. Get your pen. You spelled *birthday* and *yawns* and *tongue* wrong." She showed him how to correct them.

Dev scribbled the changes, turned to ask Mom about the address. She had disappeared. The bathroom door was closed, and Dev heard the unmistakable sounds of someone else heaving.

"Now look what you've done!" Nikki stormed. "That cat mess made Mother sick!"

"I don't see why. She didn't eat it."

Mom came back. She looked shaky, but at the same time secretly pleased. "Nikki," she said, "an upset like mine isn't sickness. I'm going to have another baby."

"A baby!" Dev and Nikki hit the words in chorus.

"Yes. I went to the doctor this afternoon to be certain. He said no doubt about it."

"When?" Nikki asked eagerly.

"Sometime next April."

"Are you pleased?" Nikki sounded as old as Grandmother, Dev thought.

"Very!" Mom smiled happily. "Dad will be, too. I hope both of you are."

"It'll be fun!" Nikki danced around the room. "Imagine having your own sister to baby-sit!"

Dev stared at his mother. Sister, nothing. This baby could be a boy. If it was, that meant he wouldn't be the Only Son any longer. And if the kid turned out smart, they'd stop expecting so much of *him*.

"Dev?" Mom asked. "You haven't said anything yet. Do you mind?"

"No. It could turn out pretty good."

"Well," Mom corrected.

"Well. Hey, that reminds me—I left the hose running when Nik started screeching!" He rushed out to turn it off. A wide lake of water filled the grass around his bike. He sloshed around in it and took great splashing leaps just for fun.

Next door, Mrs. Thornton was up from her nap and out watering her zinnias. Dev ran to see her. "Did you have more than one son?"

"Only one." Her eyes glazed in that faraway look. "Did I tell you I got a letter from him yesterday?"

"Yes'm," Dev said, but she told him about it again, anyhow. About Roger's trip abroad, what he'd written from Venice, and the meals in Paris. "Imagine!" she said. "All that rich food! I don't see how he could eat it!"

Dev laughed. He told her about Shadow this afternoon, and Mrs. T laughed, too. That was one fun thing about her. She could always see what was silly in troubles like that.

"Be sure to tell your father about Shadow," she said, wiping her eyes. "But *after* dinner!"

"Why, I'd never tell him that at all if I could help it."

She looked at him, surprised. "Why not? I think he'd like to know about your experiment."

"He'd think I was trying to poison Shad."

"Why would he think a thing like that?"

Dev hesitated. But this was only Mrs. Thornton. "He just doesn't trust me, that's all. He always expects me to do the worst."

Dev thought Mrs. Thornton hadn't heard. She moved fussily along the garden, dragging the hose after her, soaking marigolds and snapdragons and filling with water the craters of dirt Dev had raked up around the roses. Only when she finally had circled the garden and turned the hose off did she come back again to where he lay on the grass petting Boon.

"Devlin," she said, and there was a special note in her voice that made him sit up. "Don't ever forget. 'It matters not what you are thought to be, but what you are.' Publilius Syrus."

"Yes'm," Dev said. That was one of those old guys she was always talking about. He wondered where she learned all those goofy sayings. That was one of the goofiest. Because it did matter what people thought of you. Here he was, perfectly innocent, not doing half so much harm as Walt and Jim killing bees, and everybody thought he was a trouble-maker.

Just as Dev expected, Dad jumped all over him for mis-treating Shad.

"When will we ever be able to trust you?" he thundered, and Dev's restriction to the neighborhood stayed put.

chapter V

Hidden Evidence

September came too quickly for Dev. Labor Day spun past, hot, dry, and heavy with the prospect of school the next day.

The last few weeks since summer school let out had at least given him plenty of free time, even if he couldn't roam. He'd been able to work regularly for Mrs. T and mow a couple of other big lawns on the block. They were both $2.00 jobs. His savings had zoomed, his spirits with them. Their new baby was sure to be a boy. His parents would have a better son to fuss over then, and he'd be really free to duck—after nine more months of torture in sixth grade.

"Remember," Mom said, that first Tuesday morning, "it's a new beginning."

"It's also a new chance, with a new teacher," Dad said. "Make the most of it, Devlin."

He felt so pushed he burst out, "Why does everything have to be new in September? I'm not new. I'm eleven years old. That's *old*. Gee whiz. You'd think a guy was a refrigerator or a car, or something, and had to be stamped out for school brand-new every year!"

"Oh, Dev, why do you always say such peculiar things?" Mom asked.

"Because I'm peculiar!" Dev stalked out. Angrily, he slapped notebook, ruler, glue, crayons, and scissors into a plastic bag, dumped the lot in his bicycle basket. He'd been right. Summer school hadn't changed things a bit. He felt just as stupid as before all that extra work.

He rode alone to the same prison he'd hated all last year, all this summer, and would hate the coming year, too. Only difference was, his class met in a different room at the end of the hall.

He walked in, and there stood Mrs. Vogel. New teacher, nothing. After summer school, she already had him figured for dumb. Yet she smiled and said, "Glad to see you, Dev!"

"Teacher's pet!" Jim hissed.

Walt rapped the desk in front of him. "Sit here!"

But Dev slouched to the back. Let him get as far from Jim and the teacher's desk as possible. Not that Mrs. Vogel was so bad, but teachers always asked questions of people they noticed. Up front was too near being noticed.

He collapsed into a back seat across from a new girl. If he'd known she was a girl, he'd never of sat there, but her short boyish haircut and plaid shirt fooled him from a distance. When Mrs. Vogel announced they would keep the seats they'd taken "for the time being," it was too late to move.

Twice, Dev caught the new girl smiling at him. He tried not to look her way again.

Prudence Pirkle soon made it plain she was not to be ignored. She offered Dev pencils when he forgot his. She eagerly loaned him paper when his ran out. In the midst of reviewing big numbers and where to put commas in millions, she set up a game nobody in the class could ignore.

Prudence's corner seat guarded the sink and water cooler at the back of the room. She began to charge money for the privilege of reaching the sink safely.

At first, she demanded—and got—pennies. When she upped the price of a drink to a nickel, nobody would pay. But nobody wanted to tattle on Prudence, either. She had a mean foot. She'd wham it out in the aisle and flick it back so quick the teacher wouldn't see her. But one of the kids would be heading for the floor, while Prudence looked on innocently. If the victim was a boy, she helped him up.

"Please be more careful!" Mrs. Vogel would urge. One day when Jim Rothman stumbled, Mrs. Vogel actually tried to reassure him. "You boys are growing. It's natural to be clumsy, but that will pass."

The system worked so well Dev wished he'd thought of it. He had to admire Prudence. For all her round-cheeked, big-

eyed, dumb look, she was smart. She didn't trip anyone so often it made Mrs. Vogel suspicious. But the class never knew, when they entered the danger zone, who would get the foot next. Clearly, Prudence had to be paid. Besides, it was fun. The class soon tired, however, of contributing pennies to her zipper pencil case. At recess, out on the playground, muttering grew among Mrs. Vogel's sixth grade.

Dev amazed himself by coming up with the solution. The big numbers in arithmetic gave him the idea. Pennies were all right for someone who thought small. Pru, as toll-taker, made it plain she had ambitions. Why not pay her play money—in huge amounts?

Some kids rushed home and raided their Monopoly sets for fake money. Dev and a bunch of others began to manufacture money in class.

Whenever Mrs. Vogel wasn't looking, they eased a few

sheets from their assignment notebooks, scribbled numbers in bigger and bigger sums, and quietly tore the "bills" apart.

Prudence was pleased with her new take. In one exciting day, a Friday, she shot from four cents to $3,456,272,108 profits—on paper, of course. Attendance at the drinking fountain picked up.

"My, this class is thirsty!" Mrs. Vogel said. "I'll have to limit each person to one trip in the morning and one in the afternoon."

Everybody burst out laughing. She arched her sandy eyebrows. "What's so funny?"

"Trips!" Walt choked out, and everybody howled again. All but Pru. She kept a straight and apparently puzzled face.

The teacher rapped a pencil. "I suppose Friday afternoon has set you off. But we still have work to do." She paused. "Devlin, what are you scribbling in your notebook?"

Dev closed it quickly. "N-nothing."

"Let me see." Mrs. Vogel held out her hand.

Dev rose and handed her the notebook. Maybe she wouldn't find the page. She leafed through his assignment in social studies, read the page numbers for arithmetic, and sighed.

"No wonder you don't get your work done right, Dev. You've listed the assignments wrong for Monday!"

Dev reached for the notebook. "I'll fix them!"

She was still turning pages. She came to the mass of numbers. "What's this?"

"I was—uh—just practicing big numbers. You know. For arithmetic."

"Hm. That's a new enthusiasm for you." She looked up.

Everybody sat still as turtles with their heads pulled in. "Jim, let me see your notebook."

Jim passed his up. She opened it, found numbers there, too. She checked several more notebooks. Her eyes narrowed. "All right, class, what's the game?"

Every boy sat still, but one girl, turned chicken by Mrs. Vogel's glare and silence, spilled everything.

"So that's it," she said. "I thought the accident rate in that corner was unusually high. Do you realize, Prudence, that someone might have been badly hurt?"

Pru turned as red as the sun setting behind a dust storm.

Mrs. Vogel went on. "How many of you have numbers in your notebooks?"

Twenty-seven out of thirty, grinning at each other, raised their hands. Only Pru, Walt, and the tattletale didn't. The only reason Walt didn't, Dev knew, was that he'd forgotten to bring his notebook today.

Mrs. Vogel seemed to be debating with herself. "Well," she finally said, "you *did* get extra practice writing large numbers. That's good. And since no one was hurt, I suppose the game was harmless. However, it involves the same acts which, at adult level, are called threat and bribery. Do I need to remind you that both are considered crimes?"

Her question hung over the silent class. Dev studied his hands. If his part in this got home to his father, Dad would never take it for the game it was. He'd call it misbehaving in school and probably land all over Dev for not paying attention to his studies.

"I'm sure you didn't really mean harm." Mrs. Vogel swept the class with her gaze. "Prove you didn't by stopping this game. If I find one more bribe demanded or paid, the persons involved will answer to me. Is that clear?"

The whole class relaxed. No punishment this time!

"Devlin, please stay after school."

"That's not fair!" Dev yelped. "Everybody else—"

"It's not for that," Mrs. Vogel said quietly. "I want to make sure you have your assignments correct."

After the last bell, Dev watched the class file out. Why did everybody pick on him? It wasn't fair! The rest of the kids didn't hate school half so much as he did, yet he spent more time here than anyone else!

Mrs. Vogel not only wanted to check his notebook, but also planned to go over a batch of papers, including the last science test. "It's all right. I phoned your mother and told her you'd be late."

Dev settled down for a long boring session.

"Look," she said, when they reached his science test, "I know the names of bones aren't easy to learn. They sound odd because they're Greek and Latin words. But if you make up your mind, you can remember them."

"No I can't," Dev said. "I studied for that test, and I can't."

"You must," she said, "or I won't be able to pass you for the unit, Dev. You're close to failing, you know, even with the progress you made in summer school."

"I don't care," Dev muttered to the floor.

"I do." Her voice was brisk. "Your parents do. And down deep, I think you do, too. No, wait! Don't answer yet. Let me show you a simple memory trick. See this upper bone in the arm?"

Dev looked at the drawing on the mimeographed sheet. He had left that bone blank. A big red check scarred it.

"The upper bone is the humerus," Mrs. Vogel explained, "and it's easy to fix that name. Show me your funny bone."

Dev touched his elbow.

"Right. Now the humerus is just above the funny bone. Get it? H-u-m-o-r-o-u-s is a word meaning 'funny,' and the humerus is just above the funny bone."

"Did they plan it that way?" Dev asked.

"No. Actually, the name for that bone comes from a Latin word *umerus* meaning 'shoulder.' It's close to that, too, but much easier to remember by its nearness to your funny bone."

"O.K. I get that," Dev said. "But not that!" He pointed to the two parallel bones in the lower arm. He had written "radius" and "ulna" right, but put them on the wrong bones. "There's no way to remember that!"

"Just use the same association trick," Mrs. Vogel said, "except now fit it to these bones and names. What letter does ulna begin with?"

"U," Dev said.

"The ulna, the inside bone in this position is closer to *you*. You and *u*, see? It's a silly pun, but it works."

"Hey!" Dev stared at the sheet. "The radius has 'us' in it. That means somebody else, farther away from me, so I can remember that's the outside bone!"

Mrs. Vogel sat back. Her face had looked tired. Now it lit up. "You've got it! Of course, there's much more to learning than memory tricks, but this is a start. Now, what about the carpals?"

Dev studied the bones nearest the wrist, where Mrs. Vogel had written in the word he couldn't recall on the test. "I'd use them driving a car!" He looked at the next ones. "Metacarpals!" he groaned.

"*Meta* means 'between' or 'beyond,' " Mrs. Vogel suggested. "If you can remember the carpals, and then the word for beyond—"

Dev shook his head. "Too hard. But when I *met a* man, I'd shake hands with him, wouldn't I? And the metacarpals are in the hand-shaking part."

Mrs. Vogel stood up. Looking as if someone had just given her a present, she handed him the papers. "Re-test next week on this section. I'm counting on you, Dev, to know it cold!"

"O.K.!" Warm and leaping, Dev left school. Studying wasn't so bad when you could see how to do it. He decided to check Fort Rabies. It was late, but Mom knew he'd been kept after school. She wouldn't worry.

Certain that kids had knocked the fort down by now, but hoping they hadn't, Dev dashed over the hilltop. The fort still stood! He stepped inside. With a feeling like ginger ale bubbling along his spine, he saw a small neat pile of sticks, some wadded papers, and two burned matches. Someone had been here again—probably the same person as before—tried to build a fire, and stopped. Maybe frightened off. And no telling when, because Dev hadn't been here in weeks.

Should he tell the police? Yet the fire hadn't been lit. Dirt was carefully piled up around the sticks to keep the fire from spreading. Wouldn't someone crazy about setting fires have tried to burn the whole fort down in a huge blaze?

He stood for a long time considering those sticks. If he told the police, they'd probably notice the same thing about how carefully the fire had been built, and just laugh. Or they might think he'd done it, then reported it to get attention. Some people who weren't just right in their heads did things like that. And the last thing he wanted was to be thought peculiar that way too. He'd better just kick this apart, so no one would ever know.

He had pitched the last stick out into the grass and was smoothing dirt over the matches when he heard a noise. He ran out just in time to see a flash of blue jeans disappearing over the crest. It looked like Jim from the back, but Dev couldn't be sure.

He raced toward the top of the hill, fell, got up, and ran again. Whoever it was had disappeared. Low brush, wild barberry, long heaps of bulldozed trees lay between him and the suburb. Plenty of cover for a kid to hide and dodge, till he was safe down in the streets. Even if he caught Jim at the foot of the hill, Jim could claim he'd been playing there since school.

Dev turned back to the fort. All trace of the planned fire was gone. Since someone else was coming here, though, he'd better take his things, or they might be gone the next time.

He collected the rabies tag, the milk carton of fossils, the two feathers. He ducked back out. High overhead, heading west, a jet left its white pipe cleaner trail across a darkening sky. The sun, setting earlier now, pulled its warmth down with it. Dev shivered. Next year, he wouldn't be here to build a fort, or sit through summer school, or hide firewood so no one could suspect him . . .

chapter VI

Bad Break, Good Turns

Indian Summer hung on bright and warm as September burned into October. Most mornings were white with fog, but every night escaped frost. Luckily for Dev, grass grew long in the dampness and still needed cutting every week. Zinnias still blazed in Mrs. Thornton's backyard, while up on the hill, uncut slopes kept breaking out in small white asters, dandelions, sulphur butterflies, and new mullein rosettes. Dev liked to stoop and run his fingers from tip to base on the mullein's furry leaves. The fur rubbed backwards, just like Shadow's ears.

Dev was free—well, partly free—to roam again. After he brought home an A in art because he'd drawn a goldfinch landing on a purple thistle, and a B in science because he'd turned in a report and drawings of a frog's life cycle the way he'd seen it in the creek, Dad finally, one Saturday morning, lifted his "stay-in-sight" order.

"You may play on the hill on weekends," he said. "But no matches, and leave the house only when your home jobs and Mrs. Thornton's work are done."

"O.K.!" Dev was too happy to care about these small restrictions. He slid across his room, picking it up, firing laundry into the clothes hamper with long shots, kicking his hard shoes under the dresser. He wouldn't need those till Sunday—and that was almost a whole day of play away!

Finding the door shut at Mrs. Thornton's, he twisted the bell. Boon barked furiously. Dev wondered if Mrs. Thornton had taken one of her rare trips to town in a taxi or with a friend. But he hadn't seen anyone drive up this morning.

He had turned to leave the porch when the door opened slightly. "Who is it?" Mrs. Thornton almost sang.

"Dev."

"Who?"

"Devlin!" He tried to peer through the curtains at the side. She must be able to see him. Why all the mystery? Was she playing some game?

She opened the door wider. She looked queer, and her hair was mussed. When she smoothed back a strand, Dev noticed what made her face look so different. She wasn't wearing her glasses.

"I'm sorry." She gave a little laugh. "For a minute, I thought—I hoped—it might be Roger. You know. When he was your size."

Dev wondered if not wearing her glasses made everything look small. Or was she pretending? Maybe he just hadn't heard her straight. Oh, well. More and more the past weeks, what she said didn't make sense. "Any errands today?" he asked quickly. He almost hoped there weren't.

"No, but I wish you'd come in a few minutes." She opened the door wide and stepped back.

Dev hesitated. If she didn't have anything for him to do, why didn't she let him go? Gee whiz, he didn't want to work that much! But she might have some job inside.

He entered, and stooped to pat Boon, to cover the way his

nose always crinkled when he first smelled her house. Old houses always struck him with a smell half-good, half-bad. Mrs. Thornton's house smelled especially strong of the mixture—old polished wood, left-over baking, dusty carpets, damp earth in pots of African violets, yellowing newspapers piled on the stair landing, and carrots withering in the bin down cellar. The smell hit strongest at the front door. By the time he reached the living room, Dev didn't notice it.

Mrs. Thornton led him to the round marbletop table by the windows. "I've broken my glasses, and I'm anxious to find a particular quotation. Could you help me for a few minutes?"

"Sure," Dev said. "If I can."

"It's not hard." She handed him a thick red book with "FAMILIAR QUOTATIONS John Bartlett" stamped on the cover. It was so heavy he almost dropped it.

"The passage I need is by George Moore. I want to send it to Roger, but I can't find it without my glasses. I know it begins 'A man travels.' "

Dev opened the book. It was full of short quotations—over a thousand pages closely printed. "I don't see how you can find anything in this book!"

"The index. Try the index," she said impatiently. "In the back."

Dev turned to the back. Just the index alone was as thick as some whole books. Words like "eye" and "life" and "men" had hundreds of entries under them. For ten minutes, he tried to find "A man travels." It wasn't under "a," or "man," or "travels." "They must of left it out," he said.

"It's there. I know it's there. Oh, I'm vexed! If I just had my glasses!"

"Couldn't you look up the guy who wrote it?" Dev asked.

She snapped her fingers. "Of course! The front index! Now why didn't I think of that? 'Nature and Books belong to the eyes that see them.' Emerson."

"Who wrote the part you wanted?" Dev reminded her.

"Who? Oh! George Moore!"

In seconds, Dev found it. He read aloud, " 'A man travels the world over in search of what he needs and returns home to find it.' "

"Write it down for me, will you?" Mrs. Thornton handed him a pen and card. "Then I'll just slip it in my letter, and you can mail it for me. Isn't it funny? My son gave me this book years ago. And here I am, trying to give him back a passage from it."

"Yes'm." Whoever heard of making a gift of words? Some gift! Just the same, he copied every word carefully, trying to get the spelling correct. She wouldn't be able to see the book to check it. When he finished, he asked, "Is this where you get those things you're always saying?"

She patted the book. "I open this almost as often as my Bible. It holds so much. So much! Listen, you know how you're always escaping to your hill?"

"When I can. I was going there this morning." Dev hoped she'd take the hint. She didn't.

"Other people have felt much like you before. In both prose and poetry—"

Dev made a face. He couldn't help it.

"You don't like poetry?"

"I can't stand it." Mrs. Thornton was the one person Dev could answer honestly. She never got mad. "Poetry sounds crazy to me. Real creepy."

"Some of it is supposed to—like Poe's. Read properly, *The*

Raven should scare the bejabbers out of you! You've got to give me a better reason than creepiness for hating poetry."

"We-el. . . ." Stopping to think, Dev found himself enjoying the argument. Why couldn't his father listen the way Mrs. T did? "Half the time poetry doesn't even make sense!"

"Ah!" She sat back and beamed. "All you have to do is listen to what poetry tells you about what you already know."

Dev laughed. "Why read about something I know already?"

"To have it pointed up, made clearer, confirmed!" She was getting excited and running her words together. "I know one I'm sure you'll like. Turn to page 136."

Dev stared. "You even know page numbers?"

Mrs. Thornton laughed. "I told you I used that book a lot. My memory plays odd tricks. I can recall silly little things like numbers, but important things I often forget. Look for the line that starts 'By all means.' "

Two lines down the divided page, Dev found it. 'By all means use sometimes to be alone.' He read the words again. Whoever this guy Herbert was, he had the right idea. "I never knew anybody else felt that way," he said aloud.

"And he lived in a different country, three centuries ago. You have quite a lot of company on your hill, Devlin."

He looked up quickly. What did she mean? He hadn't said a word about the kid spying on him. But Mrs. Thornton wasn't even looking at him. She was gently scratching Boon's ears with the tip of her cane.

Dev cleared his throat. "Want anything else copied?"

With an effort, she got up. "Not today. But would you do

some more for me sometime? I notice you printed the passage for Roger. I like that. It's easier for me to see."

"Sure, sure." Dev edged for the door. If he didn't get going, the whole morning would be gone.

"And thank you for mailing my letter. Tell me, is the address clear?"

Dev read her shaky hand. "Mr. Roger Thornton, Diagonal 6, 17-87, Guatemala City, Guatemala. Sure, it's clear," he said. "What's he doing there? I thought he was in Paris."

"He was," Mrs. Thornton said, "but you know how he loves to travel. He had business in Guatemala, and he's stopping with friends." She pressed a quarter on Dev. "For helping!"

He didn't think that was fair. He hadn't done much, but she began to get upset, so he finally took it and left.

Outdoors, on the way to the mailbox, he looked again at the address. What funny words. Diagonal—was that a street? And 17-87. That was the year of the Constitutional Convention in Philadelphia. Dev laughed. Mrs. Vogel's memory trick worked so well that he remembered dates even when he didn't have to cram for tests.

He wondered why Mrs. Thornton's son didn't come home. She was so old somebody really ought to be with her all the time. Maybe he should take down this address.

Still, it wasn't any of his business. Why butt in? It would probably land him in trouble for copying someone else's mail.

Dev tossed the letter in the box, made sure it had fallen down, and headed for the hill. Maybe today he could find some clue to whoever was building fires at his fort. He was pretty good at noticing little things. What fun it would be to solve the mystery alone—and prove it to Dad and the police! To make sure no one saw him, or followed, Dev took a long circling route and came up the back way to the fort.

Dev leaped the outer wall of brush he'd piled around the fort. He stopped to check for footprints or signs of freshly broken weeds. He couldn't find a thing. Cautiously, he poked his head into the open doorway before entering.

The dirt still lay unmarked where he'd smoothed his sneakers over the fire site. No new fire had been burned, or even built. He had to laugh at his own disappointment.

And suddenly, the whole thing seemed babyish—sneaking up here to catch some firebug who was probably just a passing tramp or a little kid at play. And fussing to keep a make-believe fort built up, when it was more fun to watch real ants carting out real grains of dirt to clear real passages.

Deliberately, Dev turned, knocked down one of the upright stakes by the door, and ducked outside as one end of the curved arch dropped. He kicked out the other support. The arch crashed to the dirt. Dev butted his shoulders against the side walls, and they tumbled on each other. The fort fell into a heap, its room shape gone. Now it was just a pile of tangled brush and branches.

He climbed to the top of the pile. It scratched his legs, but he didn't care. From here, he could reach an upper limb in the apple tree. He swung himself up to it. From his new viewpoint, he gazed down over farmlands tawny with dried corn, up into a blue sky that held clouds curdled like cottage cheese. The sun was warm on his back. A goldfinch, in swift dipping flight, crossed from the willow down by the creek to an elm. An English sparrow landed on a branch near him. Dev held so still, the sparrow swiped its bill several times on the branch to clean it before he saw Dev and flew off.

Looking up, Dev saw several small apples hanging on the upper branches. His mouth watered. This tree hadn't been sprayed, but the apples were good—when he could find a clear bite. He stretched, pulled an apple off, and bit. Ugh! A worm!

He spit it out, pitched the apple, and reached for more. They were wormy, too. Unable to eat them, he started a game of firing the apples to the ground below. Most of them smashed, turning the earth into spots of apple butter, but one larger, firmer apple rolled to a stop undamaged.

Dev climbed down to a lower limb. It was just high enough off the ground to make a dandy swing and drop. He tried it cautiously at first, then harder. The limb was big for his hands to grip, but by launching himself from a slightly higher branch, Dev could take two big swings. Back! Forward. Jump! Two swings worked so well, he decided to try for three.

Dev caught the branch and hurled himself forward with extra force. His hands slipped. He was soaring through space, his feet straight out in front of him. When he landed flat on his back he hit something hard. He heard the clear snap of a limb. He got up slowly, trying to hurry, afraid that the broken limb would fall on him.

It was still in place, unbroken, bouncing a little from his jump.

Dev's head whirled. His stomach felt queer. He looked down at his left arm. It seemed to be wavering back and forth, retreating into the ground before him. Yet he hadn't moved it. It hurt too much to move.

Dev shook his head, sat down. He laid the silly useless thing across his lap, and fought for breath. Beside him, right where he'd fallen, the big apple that had escaped squashing when he

threw it now lay split in two. He must have fallen on it. He hung his head, trying to clear it of shimmers.

"Whatcha doing, Mr. Mysterious?" somebody yelled. "Watching ladybugs?"

Dev lifted his head. Jim stood at the top of the hill, laughing as usual. Walt, puffing behind him, frowned.

"You look greener than a frog, Dev. You sick?"

For once, Dev was glad to see the pests. "I think I've broken my arm." His voice seemed to be coming through a cardboard tube.

Walt rushed toward him, scrambling over the brush. "Hey, this is neat! We learned what to do in Scouts. Plenty of poles around, and we can use our shirts for a stretcher!"

"It's my arm, Walt. My legs are O.K."

Walt's chubby face flattened. "Well, anyway, an arm is something," he said after a second. "Gee, maybe I can get a merit badge out of this! First we splint it, then we plop it in a sling!" He grabbed a stick from the pile and began ripping off his shirt.

Dev stood up, cradling his left arm like a hurt puppy in the other. "I don't want my arm messed with up here. I can get home—if you guys will go with me and see I don't pass out."

"Hero, huh?" For once, Jim sounded more scared than bullying.

Walt and Jim walked down on either side of Dev. They made a slow, silent group. Every inch downhill, every curb, every step forward on the smooth sidewalk jolted Dev's arm. He walked head down, trying to make his steps as light as possible. His arm felt numb. He had to stop and be sick.

"Don't you want me to phone your mother?" Walt asked. "I can call from somebody's house."

Dev shook his head. If he spoke, he'd be sick again.

Mom saw them coming. She ran out to meet him and helped him up the steps. It seemed no time, and yet a long dizzy hour, before Dad squealed the tires in the drive and then, with Mom, took him to the hospital.

They waited where the X-rays were taken. The room went back and forth in a blur.

"It's broken, all right." Dr. Strauss bustled in cheerfully from the developing room. "Want to see your X-ray, Dev?"

He managed a grin. "Sure."

Dr. Strauss led him into a room so little that Dad, Mom, and the nurse crowded it. They moved aside to let Dev see the lighted picture.

It seemed funny, looking at your own bones up on the wall. Dr. Strauss pointed with his pen. "See this long upper bone? It's a clean break, clear through."

Dev began to laugh.

Mom put out her hand. "He's hysterical!"

"No, I'm not." But Dev couldn't stop the silly laughing. "I just think it's funny. I broke my humerus!"

"So!" Dr. Strauss's black eyebrows climbed above his glasses. "You know your bones. What's this—and this?" Quickly, he pointed to the two lower arm bones.

Dev studied their positions. "Turned that way," he said, "the upper one's the ulna. The lower's the radius."

The doctor grinned across at Dad. "Training your boy to be a doctor?"

Dad shook his head. He looked both mystified and proud. "None of my doing. Dev must have learned that in school."

"Mrs. Vogel showed me how—" Dev's voice trailed off. He was going to be sick again.

"This way." Dr. Strauss put a firm hand under his good arm. "We'll have you set before you can say 'thoracic vertebra!'"

Dev stayed in the hospital two days. With no cast over the break, just the weight of the lower arm cast pulling the bone into position, the doctor wanted to be sure he stayed quiet. It wasn't bad after the pain wore off. He slept a lot, even if they did prop him up in bed to make him sleep sitting up. The nurses joked about the boy who broke his arm on an apple.

Nikki sent in two comics bought from her own allowance. Either Dad or Mom came to see him every visiting hour. It seemed strange to have them sitting there, formal and stiff. There wasn't much to say, till Dad brought in an Etch-A-Sketch—a kind of erasable blackboard you could draw different straight or curved lines on by turning two knobs. It was simple to play one-handed. Dev and the boy across from him, who was getting over appendicitis, thought up a dandy game. Each one would draw a box, then take a knob and fight, trying to run his line into the other's box. Sometimes they got so excited, the nurses had to shush them.

Mostly, it was fun. But Dev was glad when the doctor said he could go home. The hospital air was too hot and stuffy.

"Keep him home in bed the rest of the week," Dr. Strauss told Mom. "That arm shouldn't be jarred."

So Dev had five more days free from school. Mrs. Thornton sent over a plate of gingerbread men and a ginger dog she iced to look like Boon. Tucked among the cookies was a note. " 'A man gazing on the stars is proverbially at the mercy of the puddles on the road.' Alexander Smith."

"What does that mean?" Mom frowned over it when Dev showed it to her.

"She's always saying or writing crazy things like that," Dev said. "She takes them from a book." He told her about Bartlett's *Quotations.*

"Well, I'm glad she has some company," Mom answered. "She's too old to live alone."

"Why doesn't her son come home?" Dev asked. "Are the police after him for something?"

"Why would you think that? There's nothing wrong with Roger Thornton, I guess, except he's rather odd and likes to wander by himself. He works only when he wants to . . . but there, I've said enough! Do you want anything else?"

"No." Dev would have liked some orange juice with the cookies, but he hated to chase his mother up and down stairs too many times. The baby was making her heavier now, and she puffed a little when she climbed stairs. Nothing must happen to that baby. Once Dad had another son, he'd have someone to satisfy him. Then Dev would be free to wander by himself—just like Roger.

He thought it was Mom coming back when he heard steps in the hall again. Walt poked his head in the door. "Hi! I've brought your homework!"

Dev burrowed back in the pillows. "Who wants it?"

Walt shook his head. "The way Vogel piles it on, you'll be swamped if you don't keep up. Don't blame me. Pru said you'd like to have it."

"She would!"

"And she's getting everybody to write you a note."

"Well, tell 'em I won't answer a single letter!"

Walt spotted the Etch-A-Sketch. "What's that?"

Dev told him how the knobs controlled crosswise and up-and-down-lines.

"You mean horizontal and vertical," Walt said.

"So I'm not the brain you are! You got what I meant. Here's the way we fight with it."

Pretty soon, Walt was better than the kid in the hospital. They had a dandy battle, which Walt won.

"You can draw pictures with it, too." Dev began twisting the knobs. The lines curved and snaked over the surface, and in a few minutes he had sketched a rough scene of farm, fields, trees, fences, and a wandering stream.

"Hey, that's neat!" Walt tried it. "I can't do it."

"It's easy." Dev showed him how again, but Walt couldn't master it. Dev started to erase his last picture—a meadowlark on a fence post—when Walt stopped him.

"You ought to leave that for your folks to see. It's good!"

Dev looked at the picture, then shook the Etch-A-Sketch to get rid of it. "I can draw that anytime."

"Bet you can't."

Dev picked up a pencil and drew another bird on his cast, this time a cardinal with its standing crest and black mask. "See, it's simple."

"Not for me. Well, gotta go." Walt was already at the door when Dev stopped him.

"Hey. Thanks for the homework, anyway. You—you want to play another battle tomorrow?"

"Sure. Can I bring Jim?"

Dev hesitated. Jim would spoil anything.

Walt turned red. "Come to think of it," he said quickly, "Jim probably wouldn't come. He said—"

"What?"

Walt looked at the rug. It was plain he was struggling whether to say anything more.

"What did he say?" Dev asked.

Walt shifted. "Well, Jim thinks—not me, I don't—but he's got the idea you might have had something to do with those fires last summer."

Dev rose half out of bed. "Is that what Jim is saying?"

Walt retreated into the hall. "All he said was—it was queer —no new fires were set since you broke your arm."

"No fires have been set the last two months, either!" Dev was pretty sure Walt didn't know about the one laid at the fort.

"Sure. I know. Well, good-bye. I'll see you tomorrow!" Walt charged down the stairs.

Dev lay back in bed and stared at the empty doorway. That day he had found the new fire laid, someone who looked like Jim had run from the hill. And now Jim had gone out of his way to mention that no new fires had been set while Dev was stuck in here. Could Jim be the fire setter, trying to throw suspicion on somebody else? Maybe if he'd watch him close . . .

"Stop scowling!" Nikki dumped a load of books on his feet. "Or you'll break your forehead, too."

Dev wiggled his toes out from under the heap. "What's that for?"

"To read, dumbbell!"

Dev picked one up. It was a mystery. "Hey, that looks pretty good!"

"Sure, it's good. You'd be surprised what you can find in the library."

"Aw, can it. I get too much of that from Dad and Mom."

Nikki took an apple from her purse and began twisting the stem. Her eyes were closed. With every twist, Dev knew, she was naming a letter of the alphabet. The letter the stem came off on would give her the boy's name she was bound to marry.

"Who is it?" he asked, when the apple dropped.

Nikki giggled. "Isaac."

"Isaac who?"

"Isaac Newton, silly."

"Who's he?"

Nikki hooted. "Honestly, Dev, the things you don't know! Isaac Newton discovered gravity."

"You mean things falling?"

"Sort of. Being attracted to the earth. Come to think of it, you and Isaac are exact opposites. An apple fell, plop, on his head, and he got a good idea. You fell on an apple and got a bad break."

"I'm not so sure." Dev grinned. "No school for a week. Just stay home and play with Shadow. That's not bad."

"You'll think so when you have to catch up."

"Walt brought my homework." Dev scowled at it. Yet it wasn't such a big heap as the library books. He sighed. "Maybe school wouldn't be so bad, if you could just whiz through your work like reading a mystery and be done with it."

"They never make it like that," Nikki said. "They want to torture us as long as possible. There's just one way to beat the game."

"How?"

"Get what *they* want you to learn learned as fast as possible," Nikki said seriously, "and then go ahead and do what *you* want."

Dev stared at her. For once, Nikki had talked to him not like an older, know-it-all sister, but like somebody on the same level—somebody with the same gripes he had. For being a girl, and a sister, Nikki wasn't half bad.

"Thanks for the books," he said. "Maybe I'll read one."

chapter VII

Cold Walk

Toward the end of November, for language homework, Mrs. Vogel assigned the sixth grade a special Thanksgiving composition. She asked them simply to list the things they were thankful for. "It shouldn't be hard," she said. "I'm sure you have much to remember."

In his bedroom Dev stared blankly at the blank sheet of paper before him. It had narrow lines. That meant more to fill up to make it look like anything at all. Too bad he'd run out of wide-lined paper.

The longer he stared at the sheet, the less he could think of anything to say. But he had to write something. Remembering the trick he'd used last week to write "I will not dream in class" one hundred times, he first wrote—one word under the other—every "I'm" down the page. Then he wrote every "thankful." It gave the composition a neat, even appearance. Then he started filling in the empty spaces:

"I'm thankful my Dad works (when he's at work).

I'm thankful my Mom stays home (when she stays home).

I'm thankful Shadow (our cat) plays (when he plays).

I'm thankful (sometimes) for Nikki (my sister).
I'm thankful I'm going to have a new brother.
I'm thankful I have money.
I'm thankful we have Halloween.
I'm thankful we have Christmas.
I'm thankful I have a brithday.
I'm thankful that I'm alive.
I'm thankful that I'm not dead.
I'm thankful I'm through with building forts.
I'm thankful for funnies in newspapers.
I'm thankful for movies, TV, and comics (sometimes library books).
I'm thankful for erasers."

He chewed the eraser on his pencil. Somehow, although he'd filled up every "I'm thankful," the composition didn't have a feeling of being finished. It wasn't rounded off like the last scene in a movie. He added one more line:

"I'm thankful this is the end."

There! That was done!

He handed it in the next morning.

"Very interesting!" Mrs. Vogel said. "It has some rhythm, and a definite climax. But Dev, it should have been handed in yesterday."

He shrugged. "I didn't get it done."

"Well," she sighed, "I'll have to mark it down a grade. It's a pity, because even with that 'brithday', and the over-use of parentheses, I'd have given it an A-minus. Now it will have to be a B-minus."

"That's plenty good!" Dev couldn't understand why Mrs.

Vogel was shaking her head. B-minus was lots better than the D's he was getting last year. It was even what his report card called "above average."

He tossed the paper on the kitchen counter after school.

Reading it, Mom laughed. "Dev, you get the craziest ideas!"

Nikki peered over her shoulder. "You spelled *birthday* wrong again," she said. "And how do you know our baby's going to be a boy?"

Dev cemented a sandwich together with peanut butter and pickles. "It has to be," he said calmly.

"It does not!" Nikki said, not at all calmly. "Our science teacher says a baby gets its sex from the way the chromosomes just happen to join!"

Mom giggled. "Honestly, you children! You know everything!" She looked anxiously at Dev. "Nikki's right, honey. It could be a girl."

"It won't be. It just won't. I won't let it!"

Nikki and Mom exchanged what-can-you-do-with-him? glances. Nikki might have said more, but Dad came home just then, and Mom showed him the composition. Dad read it, and then frowned, looking back at the first line.

"What do you mean," he said slowly, " 'I'm thankful my Dad works when he's at work'?"

Dev hesitated. He hadn't meant it to come out plain like that. How could he make it sound better? "Just—just that I'm glad you support our family, I guess."

"That's not what it says." Dad still frowned at the paper. "Because in the next line, you're thankful simply that Mother stays home." He looked up suddenly. His eyes narrowed. "Do you mean you're glad when I'm out of the house?"

"Now, Bruce," Mom said. "I'm sure Dev didn't mean that. You know how he's always getting things wrong in his papers."

"I'm not so sure this is wrong."

Dad let it drop, but the next day when he came home he tossed Dev a package. "I interviewed a man on the air today," he said almost shyly. "He told me about this book, and I thought you might like it."

Surprised, because he never got presents except on Christmas and his birthday, Dev slipped the book from its wrapper. It was Peterson's *Field Guide to the Birds*—a book his aunt had given him last Christmas! Should he tell Dad he already had it—when Dad was trying so hard to do something nice for once? Here he was, starting to change—and Dev didn't know what to say!

"Don't you like it?" Dad asked. "I—I sort of hoped we could go on some bird hikes together. You might introduce me to some of your fine feathered friends."

Dev finally found his voice. "Sure, I—well, you just surprised me, that's all." He raised his eyes and saw his mother's face flash quick as a stoplight from anxious to pleased. She knew about the other book—and kept quiet, too! Dev grinned in relief. For once, holding back words was the right thing to do!

"Most birds are gone South now," he said without thinking. Then he caught Dad's flicker of disappointment and hurried on. "But the ones that stay, they're easier to see with leaves off. We could go out Thanksgiving Day."

"Good!" Dad nodded.

Only when they went, it was bad. The hike started off well enough, as they stepped from the warm kitchen where roasting turkey flavored the air into a chill clean November day under gray skies waiting to dump snow. With binoculars around his neck and the new *Field Guide* tucked in his pocket, Dev led his father half a mile along the unpaved road beyond the suburb. They spotted pheasant and deer tracks in the half-frozen mud, climbed a wire fence, crossed a field where dry cornstalks rattled in the wind. Dev picked up two coarse-kerneled yellow cobs. "To get jays into our yard," he said happily.

Dad glanced around him uneasily. "Are you sure we should be in here? What about cattle?"

"They're kept way off by the barn over the hill now." Dev pointed. "We're only going as far as those woods."

"You come here often?"

"Sometimes—to run Boon." Dev didn't think his father needed to be reminded of the restriction that had kept him from here until lately.

"I had no idea you roamed so far."

"It's worth it. You'll see!" Eagerly, but quietly, Dev took the cattle trail past the hawthorns into deeper, taller woods. He showed his father goldfinches in their dull winter yellow, red-headed woodpeckers, cedar waxwings, and juncos.

"What's that big one?" Dad pointed into the clearing above the creek. "A pigeon?"

Dev gave it a quick glance. "That's a red-tailed hawk. See the color in his tail when he turns? And it's a wide tail. That means he's a Buteo."

Dad clapped his arm around Dev's shoulders. "Say, you really know your birds! How do you remember those fancy terms?"

"Aw, anybody knows a red-tail." Dev didn't want to waste

words describing how much he used Mrs. Vogel's memory system. He liked wide-tails better than long-tailed hawks. It was easy to remember Buteo, because to him they were the real beauts. But Dad would probably point out the spelling didn't match. Anyhow, why keep talking on a bird hike? You scared half the birds away.

"It can't be too easy," Dad yammered on. "You didn't know things like that a year ago."

Dev wriggled out from under the heavy arm. He'd caught a glimpse of something different. Big, gray, flipping a long tail —would a thrush still be here? But the tail was too long! He turned the glasses on it, then grabbed for the book. "Dad, I think—I think that's a—yes it is! It's a mockingbird!

"Oh, come on!" Dad sounded hurt. "I know enough about birds to know those are strictly southerners."

"Look for yourself." Dev handed him the glasses. "See the white wing patches?"

Dad took a brief look, handed the glasses back. "O.K. I'll take your word for it."

"What gets me," Dev said, "is what's it doing here so late? Do you suppose it's hurt?" He hunkered down, his back against a tree, to watch the bird. It flitted nervously behind tree trunks and into bushes, keeping just out of sight. If Dad would only settle down, the bird might come out so he could get a good look. But Dad walked a few yards further along the path, then came back, swinging his arms and stamping his feet.

"Hadn't we better be getting back?"

Dev kept the glasses glued on the mockingbird. "No, wait. I want to see what he's feeding on up here."

Dad stamped around until he'd kicked leaves into a circle,

looked at his watch half a dozen times, and finally cleared his throat. "No question, Dev, it's time. Mother will have that turkey done."

In raging silence, Dev got to his feet. Why hadn't he come alone? He could have stayed and discovered something about this stranger. Even on the winter bird count published every year in the newspaper, he'd never seen a mockingbird listed. Dad spoiled everything!

Dad tried to talk all the way home, but Dev answered in the shortest words possible. He kept up his silence through dinner. Mom scolded him for not "contributing to the conversation." Nikki jumped him for table manners. Dad just looked grim. Some Thanksgiving! At the end, Dev whisked the stuff off the table, excused himself to do homework.

In his room, he hauled out his geography. They weren't changing. They were pushing worse than ever! So add one more state on his route. Oregon was west of Idaho. If they kept this up all year, he'd be practically into Alaska!

chapter VIII

Spirited Christmas

Christmastime swamped Dev, with the mass of everything he had to do and buy. It seemed Mrs. Vogel, maddened by the idea of everybody escaping her clutches for two whole weeks of vacation, was piling work on twice as hard and twice as fast. Then there were all the Christmas presents he had to get for Mom, Dad, Nikki, and both grandparents. Every gift would eat into his hoarded savings. And he had to sing in a dumb Christmas concert.

He complained about his troubles to Mrs. Thornton. Usually so understanding, she just said, " 'Everyone thinks his sack heaviest.' George Herbert."

Dev went rebelliously to school.

"We three kings of Orient are," the sixth grade practiced over and over. Dev changed the words to a better version:

> "We three kings of oil and tar,
> Trying to smoke a rubber cigar.
> It was loaded, it exploded—
> BANG! Two kings of oil and tar."

"Devlin Bates!" Mrs. Vogel rapped her desk so hard a bookend crashed, and she had to jam it up again. "Since you think that's so funny, sing it through again right now. In front of the class!"

Blushing, Dev sang it through. His voice cracked horribly on the "BANG!"

"Is everybody finished laughing?" Mrs. Vogel sounded almost mean. Christmas spirit certainly wasn't getting through to her at all.

The class sat deathly still. You could hear the kids from the room across the hall. They were singing, too.

"The version Devlin just performed for us," Mrs. Vogel said more quietly, "is what you call a parody. An author takes a familiar work, and by changing the words slightly, makes a new and *sometimes* funny version."

Dev relaxed. Whenever Mrs. Vogel could use a Dark Moment in class to teach something, she never dished out so rough a punishment.

She finished writing the word on the board. "Everybody understand now?"

Everybody, including Dev, nodded.

"Very well. Devlin," her voice dripped icicles, "since you enjoy parody so much, write and bring me at least two stanzas of a parody on a Christmas poem tomorrow."

"I won't have time!" Dev yelped. "I've got to go downtown for presents and stuff after school!"

Mrs. Vogel wouldn't soften. "You might have thought of that before you wasted the whole class's time this morning."

After school, Dev stamped home through a light snow. Here it was a perfect night to sled, best snow this year. He couldn't sled, couldn't go downtown, couldn't even earn any money shoveling—all because of that dumb assignment!

Before he yanked his boots off, Mom said, "I'm ready to leave now."

"Can't go. Too much homework."

"But I arranged especially to keep the car!"

"Tell Vogel that!"

"Now, Dev. You know homework comes first." Mom hesitated. "Can I trust you alone in the house? Nikki won't be here till after her music lesson, and I really should get groceries if this snow is going to keep up."

"I won't even be here. I've got to write a dumb old parody. I'm going to see if Mrs. Thornton's book can make it quick."

"That's a good idea." Mom looked relieved. "And I know she'll like having you over there."

Mrs. Thornton invited him in eagerly, when she found out what he wanted. "Oh, we'll be busier than two feather merchants! We'll have a party. I've got fresh cookies and a nice hearth fire, and I'm sure we can find something!"

"It's got to be about Christmas."

"Christmas? Oh, dear, it is getting close, isn't it? Now where did I put that book?"

Even with her new glasses, it took her a few minutes to find the book. There were twenty entries under Christmas and one under Christmas-tide, but nothing seemed just right. In desperation, Dev ate four oatmeal cookies and a brownie.

"I still think 'Jest 'Fore Christmas' is a good one," Mrs. Thornton said.

Dev looked it up again. "Only part of it's here. Mrs. Vogel said I had to do at least two stanzas."

Mrs. Thornton limped to another bookcase. "Here it is. I knew I had a copy. I used to read this over and over to Roger!"

Dev flipped it open. He whistled. "It's awful long. And I don't see where to start."

"At the beginning, of course!" Mrs. Thornton turned open his notebook. She made him pick up his pencil. " 'Make something—and the idea will come.' I didn't get that from Bartlett's. I saw it in a magazine once. Rodin, a famous sculptor, said it. 'Make something—and the idea will come!' "

She was so sure, so determined, that Dev read the first line aloud. " 'Father calls me William, sister calls me Will.' Aw, what can you do with that?"

"A parody often turns things around," she suggested.

"Mother calls me Devlin, brother calls me Dev. Hey, it fits!"

"Of course it does!" She clapped her hands so briskly Boon jumped up to see what was wrong. "Go on!"

Pretty soon, thinking out loud, then writing, Dev had four lines.

"Mother calls me Devlin, brother calls me Dev,
Father calls me Devilish, but the fellers call me Nev(er).
Got a purple cat named Shad, teamed him up with dogs,
Last job they did together, they hauled in our Christmas
    logs."

"It's coming!" Mrs. Thornton chirped. "Oh, you do such interesting work in school now. I should love to go back!" She hadn't looked so lively in months.

They tackled the next two lines. With help from her on a rhyme word now and then, but with Dev thinking up the ideas, he struggled clear through to the end. The phone rang. He looked up, dazed.

"Put that last couplet down," Mrs. Thornton said on her

way to the phone, "before you forget it!" She was at his side again, breathless. "That was your mother. Oh dear, I had no idea it was so late! She's been holding supper for you for half an hour!"

Dev got up and stretched. He had been sitting, writing for so long, both legs and all the fingers on his right hand were stiff. "Well, it's done—except for copying," he said. "Thanks!"

"Don't thank me. Thank Rodin. Remember what he said. 'Make something—and the idea will come.'"

Dev let himself out. He felt pretty good. This time Mrs. Thornton had come up with an idea that worked. He could see what that sculptor guy meant. And wouldn't old Vogel look silly when he walked in tomorrow with his parody done?

Mrs. Vogel took one long look at the paper Dev handed her and pushed her chair back. "Did *you* write this?"

"Sure. Last night before supper."

Still reading, she tapped pencil against her teeth. "You must have had help."

"A neighbor helped me with some rhymes," he said, "but the rest is my idea."

She came to another line and smiled. "Yes, I can see that." She stood up, always a sign for the class to quiet. "Devlin, read your parody, please."

He cleared his throat:

"Jest After New Year's

Mother calls me Devlin, brother calls me Dev,
Father calls me Devilish, but the fellers call me Nev(er).

Got a purple cat named Shad, teamed him up with dogs,
Last job they did together, they hauled in our Christmas
logs.
Tamed a crow to set my place, since he likes shiny spoons,
Always flies straight to his work, morning, nights, and
noons.
Most every month, the whole day square, I'm help to all I
see,
But jest after New Year's, I'm as bad as I can be!

Father says he hopes that when I grow up good and tall,
I'll be a Big Success in life, and tower over all,
But me, I'd rather figure out why sparrows wear black bibs.
Are their table manners messy, or do black bibs warm their
ribs?
And why do finches dip in flight, while martins glide and
soar?
It's things like this that interest me. The rest is all a bore.
So Christmas gone and back to school is one big pain to
me.
That's why jest after New Year's, I'm as bad as I can be!"

The class burst into clapping. Mrs. Vogel joined, too.
"Hey, that's terrific!" Walt said.
Prudence glowed at Dev.
Jim scowled. "There's something queer about one of those
lines."
"Why, I think it's fine," Mrs. Vogel said, "and really much
more than I expected. Class, don't you think Dev's parody
belongs on our assembly program?"

There was a loud chorus of "yesses," plus one sneering "no" from Jim.

"You mean I have to read it?" Dev asked.

Mrs. Vogel smiled. "Right after we've sung 'We three kings' *correctly*."

Dev slouched down the aisle to his seat. No matter what you did, you landed in trouble. If you were bad, they piled work on you. If you did something right, they made you read it! You couldn't win!

Mrs. Vogel held out her hand. "Just to be safe, let me have your copy. I'd like to mimeograph it, too, for our sixth-grade newspaper."

"Poet!" Jim sneered at Dev on the way home.

Dev started to paste him one with a snowball, then threw it at a telephone pole instead. He didn't want to get into a fight. From now to Christmas, every afternoon, he needed his time at home, because what Mrs. T had drummed into him had solved his gift buying.

"Make something—" she had insisted.

Why not *make* every single one of his Christmas presents? He'd have to buy a few things like glue and construction paper, but they wouldn't cost much. He could get tin cans from Mom, and he had enough tablet cardboards to make backings. Model paints he hadn't used up, and his water colors would help, too. And dried weeds from the fields— there were still plenty sticking up above the snow—plus bark and fungus from the woods. Oh boy! Why hadn't he thought of this before? He'd hardly have to touch the money for his trip!

He tacked a big sign up on his bedroom door:

CLOSED UNTIL CHRISTMAS. STAY OUT.

THIS MEANS EVRYBODY.

Nikki saw it and penciled in the missing E.

He came out only for mealtimes, or to ask for something.

"Mom, can I have some empty frozen juice cans?"

"Mom, can I have three paper sacks?"

"Take them! I'm sure your room must look like the city dump by now."

"More like a factory—or a studio." Dev raced upstairs again.

"Are you keeping up with your homework?" Dad asked one night, when Dev stopped in the living room to peel waterproof glue off his fingers.

"Mostly," he said.

Dad frowned. "I saw Mrs. Vogel downtown this afternoon. She said you'd done surprisingly well in some things. What's this about a poem?"

Dev shrugged. "Got to read one in assembly."

"She said you wrote it. She said you did a remarkable job."

Mom looked up from the baby blanket she was hemming. "Why, Devlin. Why haven't you shown it to us?"

"Aw, you can hear it at the program tomorrow."

Mom dropped the blanket. "Is that tomorrow? Why didn't you say so? Oh, dear! Your white shirt isn't clean. And I'll have to press your good trousers."

"Oh, Mom, it doesn't matter what I wear!"

"It certainly does. I'm not going to have my son looking like a tramp up there, and all the other mothers noticing!"

Dev winced. That new baby had to be a boy! He went back to his room, but he refused to work on his presents any more that night. He shoved the weed pictures, the seed designs, the painted pencil holders, and the stone mosaics under his bed. He tried to read the bird book, but he couldn't find anything he didn't know. He settled down with two comics he'd read six times before.

Assemblies were always crummy as far as Dev was concerned. Christmas assembly was the crummiest. Hundreds of mothers came, and lots of little, wiggly, dressed-up kids who cried or asked questions too loud. Some fathers came too. Folding chairs crowded the gym. Every class had to march in by turn and sing three songs. Dev's sixth grade sang only two, so he'd have time to read his parody.

The paper shook in his hands. He wanted to be sick, like the time he broke his arm, but finally the last words were rushed through: "I'm as bad as I can be!"

Everybody applauded. Ladies leaned over to whisper and smile at Mom. Dev's stomach did a double flip when he looked over their heads. Against the wall stood Dad. He was beating his hands together and beaming! Now the principal was shaking hands with him!

Dev ducked for his room, shoving the last guy in line so he could get out of the gym faster. Back in the room, everybody buzzed around, excited. It was the final afternoon before vacation, and even Mrs. Vogel didn't try to quiet the class.

"It went very well," she told him. "I know your family was proud. I was proud too! And to think that started as a punishment!"

Jim raised his hand. "Mrs. Vogel?"

"Yes?"

"Didn't you notice that one queer line?"

She frowned. "You said that the other day. Which queer line?"

"The one about the cat and dogs."

"What's strange about it?"

"Well, maybe it isn't by itself." Jim shifted in his seat. "But you put it together with the first parody Dev said. There was an explosion in that one—and a fire in this."

Dev jumped up. "Where's any fire in 'Jest After New Year's?' "

"That nutty cat and dog team dragged in logs, didn't they?" Jim was grinning. "And logs are for fires."

"You're crazy!" Dev exploded.

"Maybe." Jim's cocky look denied it. "But it sure seems funny to me. You like fires so much you gather stuff for them —even in poems!"

chapter IX

Valentine Hearts and Headaches

"I realize, Mrs. Bates, that this three-cornered con-
ference is unusual," Dev heard his teacher say, "but I'll try
anything to help Dev. Unfortunately, his New Year's poem
was prophetic."

Mom sat at the reading table in the front corner, facing the
teacher. Dev sat four desks back and listened as the two of
them chattered up there, telling so many things about him he
wanted to crawl in the lockers and hide.

"He *is* imaginative," Mrs. Vogel was saying. "Today, he
suggested bottling the smell of mimeographed ink, because it
smelled so good when the papers came fresh from the office!"

Mom laughed. "That sounds like one of his ideas. At home,
he wants the kitchen floor re-tiled in peanut butter color, so it
won't show when he drops his bread. And last night, he asked
his father if printers could print books in glitter paint. He said
it would help when he wanted to read in bed at night!"

Mrs. Vogel joined Mom laughing. "He is reading more
then?"

"He was for a while. Nikki got him started on some books
when he had that broken arm, but now . . ."

Dev stared out the window. They talk about me as if I'm not here, he thought. And I'm not. My body's cramped under this little desk, pressing the seat. But I'm not here. I'm out on the reservoir in a boat, with the waves slap-slapping against the sides.

"Devlin!" Mrs. Vogel rapped her desk. "Please pay attention. We're trying to help you get better grades."

He shrugged. "I'm just not smart, that's all."

"You *are* smart! In some ways, I think you do exceptional work. When you apply yourself, for instance to that parody at Christmas, or your description—" She gave up. "Here, Mrs. Bates, look at this." She handed Mom a sheet from a folder.

Dev didn't need to see it to know what was there. For language, Mrs. Vogel had told them to describe some animal they knew well. Dev chose Boon.

He could almost feel his mother's eyes follow the scribbled page: ". . . he has rasin colored eyes, a white muzle, tan freckles on his nose, and black, shiney leather lips. His nose is black too. It looks like a wall plug. I guess if you pluged a toster or a vacuam cleaner in Boon, it might work."

Mom was shaking her head. She was laughing again, but wiping her eyes too. "That dreadful spelling! I don't know what's the matter with him. I never had any trouble with spelling in school."

"It is poor," Mrs. Vogel admitted. "But notice how freshly he sees things."

" 'Nature and books belong to the eyes that see them.' Emerson," Dev muttered.

Mrs. Vogel raised her head. "What did you say, Dev?"

"Nothing." Gee whiz! Mrs. Thornton had him saying that

crazy stuff too, now. Maybe he was as crazy as she was some-times—or as Jim said he was all the time.

His throat tightened when he remembered that last after-noon in school before vacation. Mrs. Vogel had given Jim a little lecture about not accusing people without evidence to back it up. She seemed to have forgotten it, but Jim hadn't. He'd stepped up his teasing on the sly, yelling "Hey, Firebug," or just "Firey!" until even one little kid called Dev that, think-ing it was his name. Dev tried either to get out of school early or to go home late, to avoid leaving when Jim could trail him.

"And look at that violence!" Mom was still frowning over his paper. "The idea of plugging in a dog! I don't know what gets into Dev. Sometimes he's so gentle, and then again—" She didn't finish.

Mrs. Vogel made clucking sounds. "Children this age often have wild, violent notions. I don't think Dev's unusual in that. But do you know of anything—" she glanced back toward him, "especially on his mind?"

"You mean worrying him?"

"Perhaps. He was doing so well for a while. I thought we'd solved his problem of attention. And now I see him often staring out the window, just as he's doing now."

Mom swung around. "*Is* something worrying you, Dev? Something you haven't told us?"

Dev returned her stare. What could he say? If he opened up, she'd think he was crazy—or guilty. And maybe he *was* guilty without meaning to be. He had made Shadow sick. He had thought of plugging a toaster in Boon's nose. And he did like to build fires. And he liked to be off by himself, which everybody thought was so strange. Better just not say any-thing.

He shrugged again. "I'm not worrying about nothing!"

"Anything!" Mom said, and sighed.

Mrs. Vogel took her turn frowning at the paper. "Well," she picked it up, "I wouldn't be so concerned about Dev, except that I'm positive he can do better. Much better. These rare flashes of good work show it. We'll just have to keep after him until he begins to put on his own pressure in every subject."

When his mother stood up, Dev got up, too. Pressure. Mrs. Vogel sure picked the right word. They could press and stamp and drive him all they wanted, but they wouldn't get anything out of it except to fire him farther West. Oh, golly. There was that word fire again. Couldn't he get away from it, even in thinking?

He went home and picked a fight with Nikki.

Mom sent him to his room. He left the door open and heard her urging Nikki to be nicer to him. "Dev is in trouble at school," Mom said. "Try to be extra patient with him at home."

Dev slammed the door.

Nikki would never be any different. She'd always be smart and mean and quick to jump him. He wouldn't be any different. He'd always be slow and queer and dumb, with violent ideas. Everybody wanted him to change, and he couldn't. He wanted everybody else to change—to let him alone—and they wouldn't. All they did was clamp more pressure on him.

His only out was to run away. It wasn't true those words Mrs. Thornton had sent her son—about a person finding what he needed right at home. You had to go away to be yourself, to feel good. This business of raising his grades, working better in school—he looked at his geography book again. Vogel had now sent him as far west as Washington and the Pacific.

He took all his money from the chest, and from the oatmeal box hidden under the bed. Soon it would be February—almost two months into the year when he'd escape.

February seemed the deadest, the coldest of all the winter months that year. In the bare, stripped woods only pin oaks hung on to their lower leaves. The trunks of the osage orange looked as dull as the mourning doves that fluttered in nervous, retreating blocks beyond their thick branches. Chickadees, though, stayed lively. In neat caps like black beanies pulled down to their eyes, they hopped tamely just above Dev's reach. He always felt better after watching them, standing quiet to see how close they'd come.

One cold morning when Dev came down late for breakfast, Nikki, between bites said, "Mother, guess what Dev did last night?"

Mom groaned. "Now what?"

"Oh, it's good. That's what makes it absolutely phenomenal!" Nik rolled her eyes along with her latest big words.

Mom eased herself down behind the coffee pot. "Tell me quickly then. I could use some good news about that boy."

"You know I couldn't find Shad last night when I went to bed? He was out and wouldn't come in, and the weather report said down to twenty. Well, Dev actually woke up, came all the way downstairs, and let Shadow in—in the middle of the night!"

"I'd of let him freeze," Dev said, "but I couldn't stand that yowling."

"I'd *have* let him freeze," Mom corrected. "But I don't think you would have."

Nikki flipped his head lightly in passing as she left. "Thanks Cat-Saver."

Dev leaped the whole way to school. The sun felt warmer for the first time. The snow lay rotting in dirty separated crystals, squshy underfoot. Cool air ran like clean water over his face. His cheeks were tingling when he hit the hot school room, two minutes after the bell.

Prudence turned eagerly from the teacher's desk. Behind her new glasses, her eyes bulged like a toad's. "Guess what! We get to make valentine boxes!"

Dev stopped. "Not again this year!"

"In your absence, Mr. Bates, the majority have voted you down." Mrs. Vogel looked at her watch.

Dev tried to keep her talking, to make her forget the time. "What's so good about valentines, anyhow?"

She fell for the question. "They're warm, thoughtful reminders to people we love, or like, that we remember them."

Dev scowled. "I don't love or like anybody!"

"Not even Pru?" Jim suggested.

Dev lunged for him. Mrs. Vogel whisked down the aisle between them. Whenever she stood close, towering over him, Dev could smell her perfume. It smelled like fresh spring clover.

"Take your seat, Dev. It's settled. Everybody bring a valentine box by Tuesday, and we'll have our party Thursday."

Dev made one more try. "Does everyone have to bring a box?"

"Everyone!" She glanced at her watch again. "No more time for this now. Take out your arithmetics."

When the last bell buzzed Tuesday afternoon, Mrs. Vogel

asked Dev to stay for a minute. Dev wondered what he'd done this time.

"You are going to bring a box?" She nodded toward the twenty-nine boxes lined up in red and white hearts and tissue fuss on the window sill. "Yours is the only one missing."

"I'm not going to make one."

"Why not?"

"It's kid stuff!"

Mrs. Vogel's eyes were a funny gray, with dark flecks in them. When she wanted, she could fix you like a hypnotist on TV. She fixed Dev that way now. "You really like to do big, adult things, don't you?"

He answered cautiously. "I think what you do ought to count for something. You know—not just be messing around."

"A valentine box can be done very artistically."

"I'm not a artist."

She smiled faintly. "Your mother told me you made some beautiful gifts at Christmas."

"But they had a use! They saved me—"

"What?"

"Oh, mostly the trouble of going downtown." He moved restlessly. The way his mother and the teacher told each other everything, no secret would be safe with Mrs. Vogel. If his family found out how much he'd saved, they'd make him put it in the bank, or a bond. He'd better sidetrack her quick. "I'll make you a deal. I'll fix a valentine box—just like the 'Emperor's New Clothes.' Mine'll be a perfect empty space!"

Mrs. Vogel just sat there looking at him. "Cheating, Dev, exactly like the cheaters in the story. Why do you always use your good brains to try to wriggle out from under? If you'd spend half your imagination tackling what you must do—"

"So I have to make that box?"

"You do. And an empty space won't work. The other children would have no place to put your valentines."

"They won't give me any I want to see, anyhow."

Her eyes grew very still, like pools of water waiting for a rock to be pitched. "What makes you say that?"

Dev turned away. "They won't, that's all."

"You may be surprised. In any case, bring your box—a real one—tomorrow. Good night, Devlin."

"G'night." He couldn't get out fast enough. He'd make the box. He'd slap together something and scribble the same valentine for everybody. He knew just what to say:

> *Roses are Wilted,*
> *Violets are Dead.*
> *Sugar is Lumpy,*
> *And so is your Head!*

He would make twenty-nine copies—no, thirty—because Mrs. Vogel should get one, too. He'd print an extra large dark one for Pru. She deserved it, being glad about those dumb boxes. Probably she suggested it!

After supper, he sloppily glued tablet paper on a cereal box. With red ink, he scrawled heart-shaped faces with tongues sticking out all over the box. When he printed Pru's valentine, he underlined, "And so is your Head." Then he wrote her name on the back.

Wednesday morning he crammed the folded papers into the cereal box, and at school he poked one down into each of the other boxes, making sure Pru got her special. There! Valentines for the lot, and his box on the sill with the rest. Now Mrs. Vogel couldn't yap at him. He'd done every last thing he had to!

Tough, tomboy Pru—the girl with the meanest foot in school—came in sobbing after recess. Everybody stared.

Mrs. Vogel bent over her, trying to find out what was wrong. Pru cried too hard to answer. The teacher made sure she wasn't hurt, then sent her to wash her face. The second that Pru disappeared, Mrs. Vogel turned to the rest of the class.

"Does anyone know what happened to Prudence at recess?"

The class looked at each other.

"I think someone teased her about her glasses," Walt said.

"Her glasses!"

"All I said was she looked like the fat end of a pair of binoculars," Jim said. "She does, too."

Pru's best friend turned on him. "You couldn't have said a meaner thing! Pru hates her glasses, anyway. I think they're pretty—they stopped her squinting—but she thinks they make her look ugly. Now you've said that, she'll be sure of it."

Mrs. Vogel walked to the door, looked down the hall.

"Pru's coming. There's no time to talk," she said quickly. "But please, class, guard what you say to her, or to anyone else. We all have secret things that hurt. Don't add to anybody's troubles!"

Pru ducked in and took her seat. All afternoon she kept her head down and wouldn't look at anybody. Most of the time she didn't cry. She just sniffled, and used up about a box of Kleenex Mrs. Vogel put on her desk.

The whole class finished the day in unusual quiet. Dev's mind didn't wander outside the classroom. It wandered inside. He couldn't keep his attention on social studies, or spelling, or science. When Pru found that valentine tomorrow, she'd be sure to take it personally. It was awful seeing a person caught in trouble like an animal in a trap, held there helpless. And all you did was poke at them with your own mean sticks.

Dev stared so hard at his workbook, the lines went blurry. He could try to get the verse back, but suppose someone caught him? They'd say it was stealing, and they'd be right. A valentine box was just like a mailbox. Should he tell Mrs. Vogel? His mind crawdaded backward from that idea. Well, what if he dropped a second valentine in—a nicer one? And signed it so she would know it was from him, and the other one wouldn't mean anything? No! Pru would think he really liked her, then. He couldn't stand that.

Aw, why didn't she stop her dumb snuffling?

When Dev dropped by Mrs. Thornton's to pick up Boon for the dog's afternoon run and his afternoon dime, he still hadn't solved the problem. Mrs. Thornton was having one of her livelier days. He decided to ask her about it. She listened thoughtfully.

"My, that is a fix, isn't it? "You're sure you can't steal it back?"

"I don't dare get caught. If I just hadn't put it in! Or if Pru wasn't such a dope about her glasses!"

"Hmph! 'It's but little good you'll do, watering last year's crops.' George Eliot—who was a woman, by the way."

"Yes'm." Dev headed for the door. He'd been wrong, it wasn't one of Mrs. T's best days. She was all confused. Imagine a woman being named George.

Mrs. Thornton rustled after him to the door. "I can't tell you what to do, but Emerson might."

Dev waited for the quotation she'd spout sure as breathing.

"Emerson said: 'Nothing can bring you peace but yourself.'"

"Yes'm." That was the last time he'd ask her for help in anything! And yet it was funny. Emerson, in some awful plain words, had dumped the job of figuring out what to do right back in his lap. If he had the brains Mrs. Vogel said he had, why didn't they work when he needed them?

Dev sat silent through dinner and started upstairs after helping with the dishes.

"What's wrong now, son?" Dad asked.

"Nothing. Got homework."

"There's a good TV comedy in half an hour, if you'd like to take a break with us."

Dev closed his door. One good thing about homework. It was an excuse he could nearly always use to get away. He sat at his desk, fiddled with pencils, drew forests with the ruler, and tried to make up his mind. Finally, he decided Pru would forget Jim's teasing by tomorrow and the comic valentine wouldn't matter, anyhow. Without going downstairs again, although he could have used a jelly doughnut, he went to bed. It was a long tossing time before he fell asleep.

At breakfast, Dev found three candy hearts turned upside down beside his egg. He turned them over and read "MY PAL,"

"YOU'RE SOME BOY," and "COMFORT BABY." "Hey! Where'd these come from?"

Nikki dropped into her chair. "Shad," she said carelessly. "He wanted to thank you for staying on night duty."

Dev grinned. Shad plus Nikki. "Thanks, Cats," he said.

He popped two in his mouth, but saved "MY PAL." When no one else was in the kitchen, he carved a letter *D* into the back of the candy heart. That could be Dave, or Don, or Dennis—all guys in the class—Pru needn't take it for Devlin at all.

He managed to get to school before anybody else and to sneak the heart in Pru's box. Maybe she wouldn't be here today, anyhow.

She was. Her glasses didn't hide her red and swollen lids. She must have cried most of the night. Everybody was careful not to look at her, which was just about as bad, Dev figured, as looking at her.

The Room Mothers had sent in fancy cupcakes and pop for the valentine party, so it wasn't all dumb. Girls squealed over their valentines. Boys hooted, and pounded each other on the back. They pitched cards they didn't want at each other.

Dev found one card in his box with an Indian on the front. "You Heap Big Brave," said the valentine. Someone had inked in a cast and sling over the Indian's bent arm. He turned it over. The card was signed "Your friend, Walt." Dev stuck that one in his pocket.

He dumped the others in the wastebasket, including one from Jim. It was homemade, too. Jim had drawn a red insect with matches clutched in every leg. Under the picture were the words, "Firebug, firebug, fly away home!"

He'd fly all right, come June, but not home. Jim would sure

be surprised when he found out, and maybe he'd remember this card.

Interested in reading his own valentines, Dev had forgotten about Pru. He was forced to remember when she slipped an envelope across to him. He thought it was just another valentine and ripped it open.

"Thank you, Dev," he read. It was signed "Your Pal, Pru. P.S. Isn't it funny we have the same number of letters in our nicknames?"

Like a kite, Dev's heart took a nose dive. He looked up. She was smiling at him and showing her braces. Behind her glasses she was opening and closing her eyes in the dumbest way. Suddenly, Dev noticed her eyelashes. They were short, stiff, and red—like Boon's.

chapter X

Dev's Choice

On the first warm night in March somebody lit a fire on the cement porch just outside the school doorway.

It was light enough that kids were playing outside after supper, and anybody could have sneaked up to the school, laid that little heap of sticks like a log cabin in one corner, and set a match to it.

"Child's play," the police admitted, but it was serious enough that Mr. Grompe, the principal, called the whole school into assembly.

The same policeman who had questioned Dev before spoke to them. "Now listen youngsters, playing with sticks is one thing, but lighting fires is serious. People and property can be hurt. If any of you saw anyone near the school last night, will you come to the office now and tell me? Your teachers will excuse you."

Back in class, Dev waited to see if Jim asked to be excused. His heart thudded so hard he could feel it pumping in his throat. He'd been out riding—just riding around on his bike—about 6:30. He'd come over here to swoop around the paved circle drive and see if any nighthawks were out yet. Jim had passed him here.

Jim started to leave his seat. Dev jumped up. "Mrs. Vogel? Can I go to the office?"

"Of course," she said quietly.

"Me, too?" Jim asked.

The teacher hesitated. "Suppose you go one at a time. Dev asked first. Wait till he comes back."

Jim plopped down again. Dev hurried out. Now he'd have to tell he was up here.

"I remember you," the policeman said without smiling. "What did you see?"

"N-nothing. I mean, I thought I ought to tell you I was up here last night early. I was just riding my bike on the drive. I didn't set any fire!"

The policeman jotted something on a pad. "Did you see anyone else?"

"Well, Jim—Jim Rothman passed me—out on the street. I didn't see him come near the building."

"What time was this?"

"About 6:30."

"You're sure?"

"Positive. I was home by seven. You can ask my folks."

"You didn't go out again?"

"Nope. I had to finish my Indian report. I did, too. Ask Mrs. Vogel."

"What about that dog you always walk?"

This guy knew everything! "I gave him his run right after school. Mrs. Thornton doesn't let him out at night till it gets really warm."

Dev saw the policeman and Mr. Grompe look at each other and relax.

"O.K. son," the policeman said. "That fire wasn't set until later."

Dev let out his breath. "How—how do you know?"

"It wasn't here when we stopped for a routine check at—well, never mind what time. Oh, one more thing. Know any kids who wear these?" He held up a dirty cotton glove.

Dev shook his head. "We wear wool mittens, when we wear anything."

"All right. Thanks, son."

Dev skidded the whole length of the hall back to class. He ignored Jim when he left to tattle. Whatever Jim said now couldn't hurt!

But Jim stayed in the office for twenty minutes. Dev began to worry about how much he could tell. Or maybe they were questioning *him*. Dev felt his scalp prickle. Jim sure had an awful funny way of turning up before or after every fire was set. And he sure had it on his mind all the time. Still, when he came back from the office, he was strutting, and threw a that'll-fix-you grin Dev's way.

Mrs. Vogel was trying to win the kids' attention back to social studies.

"Fire-building isn't anything new to Iowa," she said. "Long before settlers came, Indians lit their cooking fires all over this territory—perhaps on this very land!"

The spooky way she said it made Dev look out the window. He thought he saw ghost smoke rising under the swings, but it turned out to be a whirling dust devil.

"And once," Mrs. Vogel went on, "Julien DuBuque, who wanted to work lead mines up near the Mississippi River, used fire to convince the Fox Indians he had magic power. He told them he was going to light the water. Then, in secret, he floated oil down Catfish Creek."

"Did the trick work?" Pru asked.

Mrs. Vogel always got very dramatic telling a story. "The

waters *flamed!*" She spread her arms. "And to the end of his life in 1810, the Indians respected DuBuque as a man who could work miracles!"

"Not all Indians were scared of fire or settlers," Jim said. "How about that bunch at Spirit Lake?" He rubbed his hands. "They burned the works—cabins, people in 'em, and everything. They even scalped the women!"

"Augh!" Some of the girls clutched their hair.

Dev studied his desk. Just the relish in Jim's voice, the pleasure he took in what happened to those poor settlers— didn't that sound like a firebug? If Jim was the one, if everything he'd said against Dev was trying to turn suspicion away from himself, then wasn't there some way to trap him? Make him admit it—right now?

But Walt switched the subject. "I read in a book somewhere that one of the Indians on that raid—I think it was Inkpaduta—had a double set of teeth!"

Everybody whooped.

Prudence screeched. "I bet he looked like a shark!"

"Maybe he wasn't mad at Spirit Lake," someone said. "Maybe he was looking for a dentist to pull the extra set, and nobody would give him an appointment!"

Even Mrs. Vogel laughed. Then she rapped for order.

Dev raised his hand. "I know where there's an Indian mound."

"Where?" she asked eagerly.

"Down by the creek. You know, they always liked to build their burial mounds near water. I saw some real old ones once, when my family went to McGregor. Sometimes the mounds were in the shape of bears, or birds, or just circles. This one looks more like a circle."

"It can't be a mound," Jim said. "Who'd build by that dinky stream?"

"Maybe the stream wasn't always that small. Anyway, I found an arrowhead there once. They used to bury things like that in mounds."

"Then how'd it get out?" Jim asked.

Dev ignored the sneer in his words. "When they cleared this land for building, they straightened the creek. It's closer to that mound now, and every spring when it floods some of the mound washes away. I bet it'll be gone pretty soon."

"Can you show us?" Walt asked.

"Sure."

"Can we go see it?" Several kids turned to Mrs. Vogel.

She glanced at the wall clock that ran their school lives. "Too near lunch now, and we'll have to get permission for a trip away from the school. But I'll see about it."

Pru brushed by Dev at the lockers. "Honest, Dev, you get the cutest ideas!"

"What do you mean?" She'd been cow-eyeing him ever since that dumb valentine, and he was sick of it.

"That mound idea. I think it's cute!"

"It wasn't my idea. It was the Indians'."

Her giggle trailed him down the hall. Dumb girls. Good thing Mrs. T was old enough not to be so silly, or he'd never work another second for her, no matter how much she paid.

Mom met him at the door. "Don't come in yet. Take this lunch over to Mrs. Thornton."

"What's the matter—is she sick?"

"She sounded miserable when I talked to her on the phone this morning. Said she was coming down with a cold. I'd go myself, but with the baby due so soon, I don't want to risk catching anything." Mom handed him a covered plate. "She said to go right in."

Juggling the plate, it was hard to open the front door, but Dev made it. The house now smelled of camphor and mustard. He hardly noticed the old newspaper smell.

"In here," wheezed a voice. She was sitting in the high-backed chair as usual, with Bartlett's beside her on the marble-top table, and a crocheted afghan across her lap. Her cane was propped beside the chair. The way she looked, with her face wrinkled gray like the outside husk of a milkweed pod, she probably hadn't been up much that morning.

Dev set the plate on the table. "Want me to get silver?"

"Please." She kept her head back against the chair. Only her brown eyes seemed alive, glancing around the room, resting on a photograph, then on space. Dev wasn't sure she knew he was there.

He dug around in a kitchen drawer, found knife, fork, and spoon. Her eyes were closed when he came back in the room. He was afraid to speak, afraid to put the silver down, or leave. Maybe she'd die—right while he was in the house!

She opened her eyes, looked directly at him, and smiled. " 'Next to the very young, I suppose the very old are the most selfish.' Thackeray."

Dev moved forward quickly. If she was still quoting, she wasn't too sick. "I'll uncover your plate for you."

"No—no. You'll be late for your music lesson."

Dev stared. He wasn't taking music lessons. Then he got it. One day she had talked to him a long time about Roger and how he did anything to keep from practicing the piano or going to his lessons. She thought he was Roger again—like that other time at the front door!

He let himself out quickly, and told his mother how confused Mrs. Thornton was. Mom glanced at the phone uncertainly.

"I suppose I'd better call the doctor for her, poor thing. She shouldn't be there untended. But Dev, hurry and eat now. You'll be late for school."

He ate, but he couldn't have named what kind of sandwich or soup. So many ideas were whirling at once. There was Jim—how to catch him actually setting a fire. And Mrs. T. Wouldn't it be better to send not just for a doctor but her son, too? Dev knew the last address. It was still Guatemala City. Mrs.Vogel's memory tricks had left those numbers printed on his mind like a date: Diagonal 6, 17-87. He could write a postcard himself, not even sign it. Just tell Roger he ought to come home.

But if I do, Dev thought, munching his last cracker—if I do, that shoots my job, and almost three months' earnings for sure. Roger will come home and do all the errands. Anyhow, what good is it to be nice to people? I was nice to Pru just once—and she's been on my neck ever since.

"Now stop worrying, Dev." Mom handed him a tangerine. "I phoned the doctor. He'll see her this afternoon."

"O.K.!" Dev grabbed his coat and streaked for school. The doctor would fix everything up. Mrs. T might even need extra help while she was getting better. Now he was back to just one big problem—how to catch Jim.

chapter XI

April Fooled

The trip to the mound was a big success with the class, mostly because they got out of science to do it. Dev led the way along the creek path. Mrs. Vogel tried to make it like school, by pointing out what she called "the ecology of the region, the relationship of plants and other living things to their environment," and stuff like that. But the girls were too busy screeching over bugs and how the wind was ruining their hair, to listen, and the boys pretended to shove each other in the creek, until Walt really did fall in and had to be hauled out dripping.

"Where is that mound of yours?" Mrs. Vogel finally asked impatiently.

"Just beyond the stone bridge."

When they reached it, Mrs. Vogel really got excited and made everybody gather on top. "Dev, you could be right!"

"Looks like just another stupid hill to me." Jim kicked the dirt at his feet.

"Look again," Mrs. Vogel said. "Dev, what made you suspect this was a burial mound?"

"It isn't like the others around here. See how smooth the

sides are sloped up? It would still make a perfect circle, if the creek hadn't cut into it. And there's a depression in the middle."

"Like a doughnut!" Walt licked his lips.

"Made of human bones," Jim said, and everybody groaned.

"Hey, wouldn't this make a neat place for our class picnic?" Pru asked.

"We'll see." Mrs. Vogel shooed them back to school, after suggesting they check with the state archeologists about the mound, which made Dev feel pretty good.

For days Mrs. Thornton kept him extra busy after school. She wanted someone to help her with things while she was getting better, and paid him by the hour "to be an old lady sitter." Mostly she wanted someone to listen while she talked.

"I hate shots, don't you?" she said more than once. "I had to have two before that nasty germ went away."

"Yep," Dev said.

"I'd almost rather use a pioneer cure. Know what they prescribed for a head cold a hundred years ago? Take nine whiffs from a dirty sock!"

"Is *that* in Bartlett's?"

"Mercy, no! Here, let me show you." From a drawer, she took a yellowed newspaper clipping that listed pioneer cures. "Some of them were worse than the cold remedy. For asthma, drink a tea made by boiling a hornet's nest. For croup, rub the throat with skunk oil."

"What's croup?" Dev asked.

"Babies get it sometimes. They have trouble breathing."

"Will our baby get it?"

"Your baby!" Mrs. Thornton looked at him, astonished.

"Oh. Probably not. Anyhow, people know better what to do for croup now. Steam kettles or vaporizers—and keep the baby warm." She peered over her glasses. "What's your baby going to be?"

"A boy," said Dev. "A *smart* boy."

Dad tapped Dev and Nikki awake before sunrise on April first. "You'll have to get your own breakfast. I'm taking Mother to the hospital."

Dad's tie was on crooked, his hair stood up in back. Mom was neatly buttoned into her white coat. She looked like a pleased snowman.

"Be sure to brush your teeth," she said, just before Dad helped her into the car.

"Teeth!" Dev groaned. "How can she think of anything so ordinary when she's about to have a second son?"

Nikki turned from the eggs she was scrambling. "Second daughter."

"Son," said Dev.

"Daughter!"

"Son!"

"Oh, well. Third baby." Nikki salted the eggs. "Find me the cinnamon, and I'll make us cinnamon toast."

Dev opened the cupboard. He found cinnamon and sugar, and also a package of dry macaroni. "Hey, isn't this April first?"

"All day," said Nikki.

"That means it's April Fool!" He poured macaroni into his pockets.

"What are you doing that for?"

"I know a dandy trick!" He refused to tell her what.

Nikki frowned. For the first time, Dev noticed how much she looked like Mom. "Well, stay out of trouble. Nobody needs any extra excitement today."

Dad called just before they left for school. Nikki won the race to the phone. "Is it here? What is it?" . . . Oh." She sounded disappointed.

Dev swung himself between two counters. "It's a boy! It's a boy!"

"It isn't anything yet, dope. It isn't even here." Nikki put the phone down. "Dad said go to school, anyhow. Maybe he'll know something by noon."

Dev took off. The macaroni rattled in his pocket. At school, after gym, he waited until most of the kids were back in the room. Then he popped some macaroni in his mouth and went in.

Mrs. Vogel took one look at his swollen face. "Dev, what on earth happened?"

He put one hand to his nose and began chewing. "Oh! I think I've broken my nose. Ouch!" As he twisted his nose, sharp cracking sounds snapped from the macaroni.

"Don't! Don't!" the girls screamed.

Mrs. Vogel hurried toward him. "Come with me to the nurse's office."

Dev began to laugh so hard some macaroni popped from his mouth. "April Fool!"

Mrs. Vogel stopped in her tracks. "Devlin Bates! You see me after school!"

Grinning, Dev took his seat. Jim clasped his hands above his head in a champ salute. The class settled down, but every once in a while somebody would snicker again, and the sound would spread through the room like measles. Mrs. Vogel caught Dev passing macaroni to Walt. She made him empty his pockets in the wastebasket.

"Figure on staying longer!" she snapped.

That made Dev hesitate, but he didn't really care. He'd know by noon what the baby was. Meanwhile, he got a laugh every time he remembered how hard Mrs. Vogel fell for the trick.

At noon, the only news from Dad was, "Still waiting. The doctor says it may be several hours yet."

"How's Mother?" Nikki asked.

"She said to tell both of you it takes time to produce a champion."

"See?" Dev said. "Even Mom thinks it's a boy!"

"There are girl champions too," Nikki said calmly.

The sleepy afternoon crawled by. A little excitement was stirred up when Mrs. Vogel had to clear every boy's pockets of macaroni. She also removed a quantity from the girls' purses. She got maddest when Jim whistled "Yankee Doodle," but she didn't ask anyone else to stay after school. That, thought Dev, wasn't fair.

He watched everybody leave. They hung around in the hall until Mrs. Vogel closed the door on them.

She wasn't too mad. She even admitted it was a trick nobody had ever pulled on her before. "But Devlin," she said, socking one fist into her open hand like a man, "*when* are you going to wake up? You pull a crazy stunt like this, and the whole class follows you. I don't think a lick of work got done in here today because of your foolishness!"

"I'm sorry," Dev said. "I didn't think—"

"—through to the consequences," she finished. "You seldom do. If it weren't April Fools' Day—"

Suddenly the timing hit Dev. "Mrs. Vogel! Will a baby born today be a fool? You know—dumb, and making trouble for everybody, like me?"

It took her a second to catch on. "Of course not! Did your mother have her baby today?"

"Not yet. She went to the hospital this morning. If she has a boy, and it's an April fool—"

"That's not what April Fool means, Dev. It's just an expression from the sixteenth century, when they changed the calendar in France. They switched New Year's Day from April first to January first, but some people kept calling out greetings on the old date."

She went on talking, but Dev tuned her out. If the baby wasn't as smart as it should be, he wouldn't be free to leave . . .

"Devlin! Will you please tell me what makes you keep calling yourself dumb?"

He saw and heard her again. She was hunting through his folder of papers. He saw D's, B's, C's, and one lone A.

"Look at this!" She slapped her hand on the paper. It was his fossil report for science. He'd illustrated it by drawing pictures of fossils he'd found. "Good work like this makes me sick when you waste your intelligence. You could do superior work in everything, Dev, if you chose. You are *not* dumb. Stop hiding behind that excuse!"

Dev felt a kind of shock. She really meant what she said. She wasn't just talking to make him feel good. If it was true— if he wasn't dumb, that left just the queer, wanting-to-be-alone part to worry about. He wanted to get away to think. "Can I go now?"

Something—was it disappointment?—dragged her face down. He guessed he hadn't answered what she wanted.

"Well, no more macaroni tomorrow. Promise?"

Dev grinned. "Maybe I'll bring some candy cigars!"

She put her head in her hands. "No. No cigars, either. Just bring yourself, ready to work for once!"

"O.K." He shot for home. On the way, he passed a row of garbage cans set out for collection. On top of one, a faded Easter lily lay tipped over. Two blossoms were wilted, but one was still fresh. Dev looked at the lily. Dumped like that, no one wanted it. It wouldn't be stealing. And Mom liked flowers. She had a seed lamp going in the upstairs hall, raising seedlings for her garden. Why not surprise her when she came home?

He rescued the lily, tarnished purple foil, broken pot, and all. After letting Shadow smell the blossom, and noticing that cats—Shad anyhow—didn't like the smell of lilies, Dev placed the pot in the center of the dining room table.

He went to get something to eat. Nikki had left a note. "Baby-sitting at Collins' till 5:30. Please call if Dad phones or comes home." She'd underlined "please" three times. So she still didn't know what the baby was.

Dev glanced at the clock. He should go walk Boon, but Dad might call any second. Boon could wait awhile, and he'd give him an extra long run later to make up. Satisfied with his own excuse, Dev started banging cupboards open just to put some noise in the empty kitchen. It seemed strange without Mom in it. Somebody had to set the table for supper. He could even get potatoes started. Munching on a steady parade of peanuts, bananas, and chocolate-covered graham crackers while he peeled nine potatoes, Dev soon had a full saucepan, and an almost full stomach. There was still a hollow corner in his stomach though. He cored an apple, filled the center with peanut butter, and ate that. Ah! That did it. Humming, he skidded plates and glasses across the plastic tablecloth. Shadow purred on the couch. Both noises failed to drown the hum of Dad's car when it turned the corner and came down the block.

Dev ran outside. Nikki legged it up the drive after the car. They both hit the car door together. "What is it?"

Dad got out of the driver's seat. He looked like a rain-beaten meadowlark, his black tie yanked in an open V on his chest, his eyes about as smudged gray underneath. But he had his coat slung over his shoulder gaily, and he sang as he got out of the car.

"It is," he caroled, "a very large, rather red, somewhat noisy creature named Emily Rose!"

"A *girl?*" Dev said.

"A girl!" Nikki cried.

Dad dropped his arm around Dev's shoulders. "Did you want a brother so much?"

"I—I—it didn't matter." He rushed in the house ahead of Dad. Dad mustn't see how much it mattered. Now all his plans were ruined. He was still the only son, maybe not so dumb anymore, but different as ever. Peculiar. A lone duck dragging behind the flock. Or that marooned mockingbird he'd never found an explanation for. He was not like the rest, but now they'd keep trying to make him be . . .

Dad came in. Dev kept his head turned. "Can—May I go tell Mrs. Thornton?"

"You'd better," Dad said, "especially about the Rose part. That's for her, for all she's done—"

Dev didn't hear the rest. He ran outside again and up the walk. Mrs. Thornton's door was unlocked. He was used to going in, after knocking, ever since she'd been sick.

"Mrs. Thornton!" he called. He waited for her to answer

from upstairs, or down in the cellar, or for Boon to come pattering. "Mrs. Thornton?" Only the steady drip-drop, drip-drop of the grandfather clock on the landing answered him.

She couldn't be far away. He walked through the house and looked out the kitchen window. She was sitting on the bottom back step, hunched over as if she held a cat in her lap. Boon was curled at her feet.

Dev ran out. "Are you all right?"

"C-cold," she whispered, with her hands under her apron. "I'm so cold. I thought it was warm this afternoon, and I c-came out. And then I just c-c-couldn't seem to get up." Her teeth chattered on every word.

Dev helped her back in the house. She seemed light as a dried weed, leaning against him. He saw suddenly that he must have grown taller this year. He could look down on the top of her head! He eased her into her chair, tucked the afghan around her. After he'd fixed her a cup of tea, her shivering stopped. She was pale, but seemed all right.

"The baby's here, Mrs. Thornton." Dev told her about naming it Emily Rose.

Then she really looked warm. Her cheeks flushed pink. "How nice! A namesake! Oh, I shall have to see her when she comes home!" She stopped. Her voice lowered. "What about that smart boy you wanted?"

Dev shrugged. "Guess I didn't get it."

"Why did you want a *smart* boy?" When she was curious, the end of Mrs. T's nose quivered like a guinea pig's.

"So my Dad would have a son to turn out the way he wanted." There! The words were out in the open. Somebody else had heard them. It was only Mrs. Thornton, but Dev felt better after finally saying them.

She leaned forward slightly. "You don't think *you're* what he wanted?"

"Of course not, or he wouldn't be pushing me so much to change."

She sat back. When she was thinking, her eyelids hooded long and deep over her eyes. She looked like a small fierce turtle. "I suppose it never occurred to you that even though you might not be what *he* wanted, you could be very fine in yourself?"

Dev stared. Was she quoting something else from that book? Yet she hadn't given a name after it.

"I am not trying to come between you and your father, Devlin. He's a very fine man, in his own way. Very strong. Very steady. Very outgoing. But you are *you*." She rapped her cane. "You see, where others do not see. You enjoy quiet. You are not afraid to be alone. And I believe in a man who can see and retreat and live with himself, free from others."

"I'm not a man," Dev heard himself saying.

"You are a piece with the man to come!" She rapped her cane again, fiercely. "Believe in yourself, Dev. In what *you* can do."

"I can't do anything."

"Is telling birds in a flash nothing? Your father boasted to me about that. Is steady help for me nothing? I am daily grateful for that. You are doing a great deal, Devlin. And you will do much more as you grow. Now leave me. I'll be all right. Your father will want you home with him tonight."

Slowly, Dev took the brick walk out to the sidewalk, made a U turn, and started up the drive. He wanted a couple minutes before facing Nikki's chatter—or Dad's.

The first evening star was out. He turned to watch it climb

in a sky that shone green and clear like a drop of water. For all her fierce words, or maybe because she had used them to help him, Mrs. Thornton was too weak, too pale. She should never of sat out on those steps so long. Her mind might be O.K. most of the time, but her body shouldn't live alone now. She had the aloneness he wanted—and it wasn't good for her. Probably, if she told all the truth, she didn't want it a bit. With Roger away, the main person she had to talk to was a boy.

The one high bright star was joined by another. Was it a signal Roger should come home? Dev watched the two cold stars. He felt as cold as they looked. He should write to Roger —if he was willing to give up the chance to earn more money from Mrs. T. She'd said he could do a great deal. And this was one thing he could do . . .

"Dev?" Nikki opened the kitchen door. Warm light spilled like a corn shock across the cement. "Thanks to your start, supper's ready."

"Be there in a second." Dev ran to the study. He grabbed a postcard from the desk before he could change his mind. He wrote just four words. "Mrs. Thornton needs you." He printed the address on the front and added his own address in the top corner. He could mail it tonight, after supper—if he could forget his selfish chance to pile up cash and remember Mrs. T's face, and the way her hand looked so white on that cane.

chapter XII

Matches at Midnight

That night, Dev had a hard time going to sleep. Nikki was in her room, doing homework. Dad was already asleep. He had gone to bed, yawning, right after seeing Mom at hospital visiting hours. He'd seen Emily again, too. "She yowls like Shadow," Dad reported, "only she doesn't have teeth."

"She'll make plenty of noise when she gets home," Nikki said.

"Plenty of fun, too," Dad said, and disappeared into his bedroom.

Dev lay and listened to the house sounds, so soon to be drowned out by a baby. Nik's radio was on low, playing classical music. Once in a while, she tapped her foot in time, or blew her nose. She was catching cold. The special light from Mom's seed lamp hummed outside in the hall. It threw a violet shadow of the railing on the wall.

Dev stretched. He found his feet came clear to the bottom of the bed. What did grown-ups do, let their feet hang off the end?

He punched his pillow fatter, trying to make it more comfortable. He wished so much hadn't happened in one day. It took time to sort things out. Everything fell on top of everything else so fast there wasn't time to think.

Mrs. Vogel said he had brains. He should use them only for Good. That was the same kind of Good Dad meant—for better grades, for making a big success every place you went so everybody would notice you.

But Mrs. T said it was all right to turn your back on that. To go alone. To be different, if you wanted. And if you were different, you sure weren't going to run with a crowd.

Which one was right? Or which ones? Dad and Mrs. Vogel and Mom—sort of—took one side; Mrs. Thornton took the other. Why couldn't grown-ups get together, and agree what was right? And then tell kids? Dev flopped over and punched his pillow again. The sounds from Nikki's room had stopped. Now everyone was asleep except him.

He thought about the card he'd mailed to Roger. That was another question. Was it right for him—a kid—to stick his nose in a grown man's business? Roger didn't want to come home, or he would have, any more than Dev wanted to stay home.

He sat up and threw back the stifling blankets. By sending that card, he'd tried to stuff the same thing down Roger's throat that everybody but Mrs. Thornton was trying to stuff down his! This is what you ought to do. Do it! That's what the card really said. And he hated pressure like that when they turned it on him, hated it so much it made him want to run away and do exactly the opposite!

Feeling sick, he got up. It was too late to get the card back now. And it would make Roger mad when he got it. If he'd only thought it through before—"the consequences," as Mrs.

Vogel said. He smacked his head. Of all the dopes! He didn't have brains. He couldn't see anything for what it was.

Something scraped on the drive. Dev looked through the half-opened window. The corner of their house blocked the streetlight. He couldn't see anything but dark shadow. The scraping noise came again, louder, like wood dragged on cement. Then the crumpling of paper. The sound was coming from the window well, right under his room! Someone was trying to build a fire! Maybe he'd finally caught Jim!

Dev started to push the window far enough up to lean out. But Jim would hear it. The window didn't move easily. He pulled his hand back, tip-toed across the room. He could sneak out the back door and come around.

At the head of the stairs, Dev stopped. The consequences! If it wasn't Jim, if it was someone bigger, then he couldn't handle him alone. And if it was Jim, he should have a witness. He should call the police—but whoever it was might escape.

Dev rushed to his father's door. "Dad! Dad! Wake up!"

"Huh?"

"Someone's trying to build a fire in the north window well!"

Dad's feet hit the floor. "Sure? You're not trying to April Fool me?"

"No, I'm not. I mean I'm sure. I wouldn't fool about that!"

Dad was out in the hall and running downstairs. Dev was surprised a man as big as Dad could run so lightly. He blessed the seedling lamp for spreading its faint glow down the stairs. They wouldn't have to turn on lights and scare the firebug away.

He heard the closet door downstairs ease open, then the rattle of golf clubs. Dev grabbed his baseball bat and a flashlight and rocketed down the stair rail.

"You're not going out!" Dad whispered. "I need you to call the police."

Dev was suddenly scared. "Do you have to go out?"

"Can't see anything from inside. And the guy's still at it." Dad started for the back door. "Phone from the study, Dev. He might hear the kitchen phone."

"Can't you wait for me?" Dev whispered.

In the darkness, Dad was silent. Then, "No waiting, Dev. This is a two-man operation. I'm outdoors this time. You're indoors. Quick!"

Two-*man*, he said! Dev rushed for the phone and dialed "O." He might still get in on the capture if he hurried. "Operator, get me the police!"

"Police Headquarters, Sergeant Rothman speaking," said a calm voice.

That was Jim's uncle! And Dad was about to catch Jim! Dev steadied his voice. He told the sergeant what he had heard and gave the address clearly so he wouldn't waste time repeating it. Dev hung up and ran back to the kitchen. Soft as breathing, he opened the back door and closed it behind him. The terrace cement burned cold under his bare toes, but at least it didn't squeak the way boards would. There was that one part of him again, standing off and thinking things like that, when danger prowled just around the corner!

Dev heard a cry, then a startled sound from Dad. He dropped his baseball bat, but kept his flashlight and ran. Dad had a golf club. He might need light more. And anyhow, Dev could use the flashlight for a club if he had to.

He pressed the button, and lighted the two figures struggling by the mound of kindling and papers in the window well. It wasn't exactly a struggle. It looked more like a dance.

In his arms, Dad held Mrs. Thornton.

She was shivering, and leaned on him for support. Her eyes glittered in the glare of the light. "You should keep your house warmer," she chattered. "My namesake should have a w-warm house. 'Fire is the most tolerable third party,' you know. Thoreau."

"Mrs. Thornton," Dad held her gently. "Did you come over to see the baby?"

"That's right. Miss Emily Rose. My namesake. But I d-do think you should light the fire, or she'll get c-croup."

"We will." Dad turned her toward the back door. He signaled with his head for Dev to come.

"My cane!"

"I'll get it." Dev ran to pick it up from the window well where she had let it drop. The gold head was unscrewed. In the top of the cane was a hollow stuffed with long kitchen matches. Dev held the two parts in shaking hands. It couldn't be. She just couldn't be the firebug! The fires set at the fort, the one at school—weren't they too far for her to walk?

From both sides, arms gripped and raised him. He looked up to see two huge policemen. One was the same man Dev had faced twice before.

"I-I—"

"Don't try to talk your way out of this one, son." The man saw the cane. "Where did you get that?"

Dev found his voice again. "It's Mrs. Thornton's. I'm the one who called you. Come in the house. Come on. You'll see!"

They marched him in, keeping a grip on both arms, as if he'd twist and run from his own house. Dad had put Mrs. Thornton on the couch and covered her with a blanket. She was asleep, drawing deep ragged breaths that hurt Dev to hear.

Dad offered the policemen coffee. He stood in the kitchen doorway where he could watch Mrs. Thornton and still talk. "She didn't know what she was doing or saying. When I brought her in the kitchen, she looked around and said, 'Yes, a stove is a nice warm place for a baby.'"

"We knew about her," the policeman Dev knew said, "but we figured she was just out walking her dog."

"Boon?" Dev asked.

"She often walked him late at night, usually in that pink and green blanket."

Dad shook his head. "She has this notion she wants everything warm. Otherwise, she seems to be all right."

"She can't be the firebug!" Dev said. "Maybe she could get as far as Seldings' garage, or that pile of scrap lumber. But she couldn't walk to school, or my fort!" He told them then about finding the other fires.

"It's possible someone else set those," the policeman said. "But people can do surprising things when they aren't themselves, especially if they have a reason. Did you talk to her much about your fort, or school?"

"Some," Dev said, "and once she said she'd like to go back to school." He caught his breath. "That glove—"

"The workman's glove?" The policeman wouldn't let him stop now. "What about it?"

Dev swallowed. That glove was the last thing they needed to be sure.

"What about it?" the policeman repeated.

"She wears gloves—something like that—to pull weeds."

The policeman looked thoughtfully at Dad. "She have any relatives?"

"Just one son. He's out of the country."

"What's his name?"

"Roger Thornton," Dev said. "I—I wrote to him tonight." It seemed farther back than kindergarten. He told them how he knew Roger's address.

"You're sure of it?" the policeman asked.

"Of course!" Why did everybody keep asking him if he was sure of the things he knew?

The policeman wrote it down. "Well, she'll have steady company until he gets here."

"You aren't taking her to jail!" Dev said.

"Of course not. We'll get a nurse, or a companion out here tonight. And tomorrow, she can go into a home where she'll have good care and attention until her son comes."

"She won't like that," Dev said slowly. "Why can't she just stay in her own house? Dad, you said yourself she's all right most of the time!"

Dad faced him across the table. "She's at a stage of her life where she needs care, Dev. She *needs* it. Would you keep her from having it?"

Dev met his gaze, wanting to cry, wanting to fight for Mrs. Thornton's right to go on living the way she wanted. They couldn't shut her in, and watch over her, just because *they* thought it was right!

"Devlin?" Mrs. Thornton spoke from the doorway.

He turned. The strange glitter had gone from her eyes. Under the kitchen light, she looked old, tired, but calm. " 'You cannot run away from a weakness; you must some time fight it out or perish; and if that be so, why not now, and where you stand?' Robert Louis Stevenson," she said.

The two policemen went to stand by her like an honor guard.

Dev picked up the cane from the table. He took the matches out, fastened the two parts together again, and handed it to her.

"Just make sure," he said, and he couldn't keep his voice from wobbling, "just make sure that nurse—or companion— or whatever she is—likes to read!"

chapter XIII

Surprise Next Door

Dev's postcard returned in the morning mail, POST-AGE DUE stamped on the front. When Dad came home at noon to be sure Dev ate right, and check on Nikki's cold, he found the card.

"You forgot it costs more to send mail out of the country," Dad said.

"And I was so sure I'd done everything right!" Dev felt like kicking himself, yet he was glad, too. Now he could change the bossy words on the card. And there was more to say.

Dad shook his head. "In lots of ways, Dev, you're learning. I'm pleased. But you still have a long way to go—which proves you're like the rest of us, I guess." He was peeling carrots at the sink. "Who's that going into Mrs. Thornton's?"

"Maybe it's the police again!" Nikki ran to the front windows. She was mad because she'd slept through last night's excitement. She wasn't about to miss anything new, especially with the chance to stay home today.

"It can't be the police," Dad said. "A taxi dropped him."

"Him! I thought you meant the nurse!" Dev ducked under Dad's elbow. He saw a small dark man crossing the lawn. The man stopped to look up at the trees, then over at their house. Why, that's Roger! That's her son!"

"How do you know?" Dad asked. "He hasn't been home since we built here."

"Mrs. Thornton's showed me a million pictures of him." Dev jumped up and down. "He's back! He's back! Can I go over?"

"Of course not," Dad said. "She'll want to see him alone."

"She's not alone. She's got some woman over there. I saw her this morning!"

"Nevertheless," Dad ordered, "this is no time for outsiders. Eat your lunch."

Dev plopped into his chair. He wasn't an outsider. He'd known Mrs. T better than her own son, even, for almost two years. Hadn't he seen her practically every day?

"Stop crunching those carrots like bones!" Nikki said. "I can hear you clear across the table!"

"If it was just Saturday—or I was sick like you—here I gotta go back to school!"

"Have to go back," Dad corrected. His lips twitched. "I suppose you *could* check with Mrs. Thornton after school, just to see how she is."

Dev gulped the last of his milk. For once, Dad seemed to understand how he felt! "See you," he said.

On the way to school, he wheeled his bike across Mrs. T's front yard. Through the long curtains that covered her windows, he couldn't see anything of Roger.

Jim and Walt, on their bikes, caught up with him.

"Got any macaroni?" Jim asked. Ever since that dumb joke, he never mentioned anything else.

"You crazy?" Dev asked. "I don't want to stay after tonight!" He told them about Roger's return. He didn't say a word about catching Mrs. Thornton, but Jim knew something —at least that the firebug had been caught. Pretending he just couldn't tell any more, he had spread that news all over school this morning.

"I'm not crazy, any more than you are," Jim said. "Know what? I saw you one day kicking dirt on a fire at your fort. I was absitively posulute you were the firebug!"

"And I thought you were! You were always talking about it!"

"I was trying to trap you." Jim grinned. "We sure got fooled."

Dev noticed the careless way he said "we." Jim was buddy-buddy now, sure. But just let something happen, or let him get in a mean mood, and he'd go right back to bullying.

Walt was more of a friend—if he had a friend. Dev glanced sideways at him. Walt always rode his bicycle like a racer, leaning way over the handlebars. Lately, Pru had noticed him. She thought Walter was cute now. Dev laughed.

Walt peered around. "What's funny?"

"Thanks," Dev said.

"For what?"

"For getting Pirkle out of my hair."

Walt groaned. "Anything for a pal!"

"Aw, you two sound like a movie!" Jim zoomed ahead.

Dev managed to make it through language, music, reading, and spelling without getting Mrs. Vogel mad once. He streaked home, washed his hands and face, and climbed Mrs. T's front steps.

Roger answered the door. He wore a faded tan sweater, old trousers, and a red apron, but he didn't seem embarrassed.

"You're Dev," he said, shaking hands. "Come in. Mother was asking if you'd been over."

Up close, Dev could see he had brown snapping eyes like Mrs. Thornton's. His dark hair was streaked with gray. It seemed funny to hear him call, "Mother! Here's company!"

She was stretched on the couch, but sitting up. Her eyes sparkled.

"You look good!" Dev said, before he thought. "I mean—"

She laughed. " 'A little sunburnt by the glare of life,' I'm afraid. Elizabeth Barrett Browning. Guess what!" She seemed like a child with a secret too good to keep. "Roger is coming home to stay. He was, even before last night. We're going to build a new house up on top of Knob Hill, where we can see to every horizon! Oh, I'm so glad. So glad!"

Dev didn't know what to say. When grown-ups got all excited, they expected you to be excited too. It was nice for Mrs. Thornton. She wouldn't have to move out of her own home, or have somebody strange in the house. But maybe Roger had lied. Maybe he just happened to come home and then decided he *had* to stay. Dev sneaked a look at him.

Roger bent his head slightly toward the kitchen. "Want to help me buttle some tea?"

Dev wasn't sure what "buttle" meant, but it sounded like fun. It turned out to be just fixing up a tray with tea, toasted muffins, jelly, and oatmeal cookies. Roger took a long time doing it, all the while asking questions.

Dev found it simple to talk with this man about the best places to find trilobites and morels, about where Canadian geese wintered, and what route Monarch butterflies followed in migrating from South America. In fact, it was easier to talk to Roger than anyone else Dev had ever known. He wished he dared ask Roger how he really felt about coming home, but that was too prying.

Then Roger asked a question in a different tone. "Ever see a flycatcher?"

"The ones that fly from a tree, grab a bug, and then go back to the same limb? Sure. Plenty of times."

Roger nodded. "You really do know birds. Well, that flycatcher is me. Back to the same old station after feeding on the sights of the world."

"But you're not a flycatcher!" Dev seized his chance. "How can you be satisfied coming back—even to a new house—after all that escape?"

Roger seemed to be studying the tray. "It didn't turn out to be such escape, Dev. You know, I always used to hate the story of the Prodigal Son . . . the one who was different, who went away for excitement. It always made such a big thing out of getting the son to come home to please the father. But I learned something in these years away. Maybe it will shorten your years of wandering."

"Me?" Dev asked, surprised. How did Roger know how much he longed to get away, to do just what he wanted?

"You. You're a wanderer—in spirit, if not yet in body. It sticks out all over your conversation. You don't like to run with other kids, do you?"

In silence, Dev shook his head.

"You're a loner, just as I was. And perhaps a lot more, because you're more observant, more of a naturalist than I was at your age." He laughed. "You see, Dev, I learned plenty about you through Mother's letters. It backs up what I see now."

"But—but—" Dev had to know, even if it meant saying

things he'd never dared bring out in words before. "You hated the idea of doing things just to please your father or your mother. And now you're back to do it. How can you stand it?"

"Because I found out you can come home, and stay home, with a difference. Within yourself, being yourself. Real escape is inside people like you and me, Dev. The out is in."

"The out—is in?"

"Sure. Our answer, our way out of the trap we feel caught in, is inside us. We can lead an apparently conforming life, but inside we're free—to think, to observe as we want. Our kind can never be bored. There are people and places and life to watch. Plenty to learn, plenty to question, no matter where we're pushed. And we will be pushed. Some things we don't want to do, we'll have to do. It's no good being so different if that difference hurts everyone else, Dev."

"What—what if it hurts yourself?"

"How?"

"When you know you're different," Dev said slowly, "and you don't really like it, but you still can't stand being like the others."

Roger whistled softly. "That one, Dev, you've got to work out for yourself. Maybe you'll change some. Or maybe you'll get to like what you are. One thing sure." He picked up the tray. "I like what you are. Right now!"

chapter XIV

Homecoming

Three days later, when Mom brought Em home, Dev was busy rigging a pulley basket with his erector set. If it worked, Mom could run diapers and stuff from the shelves in the baby's room over to the changing table without taking a step.

"They're coming!" Nikki squealed.

Dev ran downstairs. Mom came in all smiles. She looked around the house as if she'd been away five months, instead of five days. "What a beautiful Easter lily!" she said.

Dev looked at the lily. He knew it wasn't beautiful. The last blossom was wilting like the others had. But he was glad she noticed it. He peered at Emily. A pink papoose in a yellow blanket, she lay in her basket, boxed with her fists, and made sucking noises for the first five minutes. Then she opened her broad toothless mouth and howled.

Shadow shot from the couch for upstairs and peace.

"Shad doesn't like her," Dev said.

"Shadow can get used to her," Nikki said.

"Well, she doesn't make near so much noise as I thought she would," Dev admitted.

"Nearly so much noise," Mom corrected gently.

"Wait till 2 A.M.!" Dad looked around. "Hey, five of us. Pretty nice!"

"Six—counting Shad." Dev went upstairs to find him. He hunted first in Nikki's room, where Shad usually went to sulk. No striped gray-on-grey cat. Dev reached under his own bed. He pulled out a spitting, clawing, flat-eared Shadow, and his oatmeal box of money. The paper lid fell off. Bills and coins spilled across the floor. Shadow chased a rolling dime out into the hall, then downstairs.

Dev stirred the heap with his finger. Quite a pile! Nearly a whole year's savings from allowance, tips for walking Boon, extra jobs for Mrs. Thornton, mowing lawns, shoveling snow, Christmas money his grandparents had sent. The last time he'd counted what was here and in the chest it was over a hundred dollars. Plenty to take him away from here—and now he wasn't sure he wanted to go.

"This your dime?" Dad asked from the doorway. He sucked in his breath with a sigh like wind in the pines. "Devlin! *Where did you get all that money?*"

Dev stood up. He faced him. "I saved it. I did!"

Dad stared at the pile with loathing, like some people look on snakes. "How? How did you save it?"

"By not spending anything for a year. Well, almost a year. Since last June!"

Dad looked at him with fear woven tight in his face like threads in a jacket. Can I believe you? Can I believe you? his eyes begged.

Dev braced for the cold accusing words he knew would come. When his father said them, when he laid the words out between them, he would have to go. Even with Roger home, he would have to. His father didn't trust him now, any more than last year when he thought his only son was roaming the night setting fires.

But why should Dad trust him? The part of Dev that could stand off and watch suddenly saw his father's doubts clearly. A son who kept to himself, who almost never shared what he found or felt—why should his father trust him? He doesn't know whether I'm good, bad, or in-between, Dev thought. And neither do most of the kids at school. I hide too much. I shut everything up inside. Something must come out, or the difference between Dad and me will go on hurting.

His father's lips twisted. Dad opened his mouth to speak, closed it again. He looks, Dev found himself thinking, like Mrs. Thornton last night. He's about to do something awful, calling me a liar and a thief, and he can't help it. But I can. I can stop him by saying more than I want to say.

Dev started to speak, but his father beat him to it.

"What were you saving the money for?"

He believed him! He hadn't accused him! Dev felt breath like fresh air rush into his chest. "I was saving the money to run away," he said, almost easily. "I don't need it now. Could I—could we use it for a camping trip maybe this summer?"

Dad's face held that rigid, glittering, frightened look for one more second. Then he dropped to his knees, to help pick up the money. "Sounds good to me," he breathed. "Where shall we go?"

Dev thought for a second. "Let's go West." He grinned. "I know the route."